TENEBRAE
A Passion

LIAM LYNCH was born in Dublin in 1937. As a child he lived in counties Cork and Limerick. After the death of his father (a sergeant in the Garda Siochana) he returned to Dublin, where, apart from stays in Birmingham and London, he has remained since. *Tenebrae* is Liam Lynch's second published novel, after the highly acclaimed *Shell, Sea Shell.* He has already won a reputation as a playwright. His plays include: *Do Thrushes Sing in Birmingham?* (Abbey Theatre, 1963); *Soldier* (Peacock Theatre, 1969); *Strange Dreams Unending* (RTE Radio, 1973); *Krieg* (Project Arts Centre, 1981).

In memory of my mother

TENEBRAE . . . 'Matins and Lauds of Holy Week involving the gradual extinction of lights. L. *tenebrae*, darkness.' *Chambers Twentieth Century Dictionary*

TENEBRAE
A Passion

Liam Lynch

WOLFHOUND PRESS

First published by
WOLFHOUND PRESS
68 Mountjoy Square, Dublin 1

British Library Cataloguing in Publication Data

Lynch, Liam
  Tenebrae.
  I. Title
  823'.914[F]   PR6062.Y5/

ISBN 0-86327-037-9
ISBN 0-86327-036-0 pbk

This book is published with the assistance of the Arts Council (An Chomhairle Ealaíon), Dublin, Ireland.

The author wishes to acknowledge the assistance of the Arts Council (An Comhairle Ealaíon), Dublin, Ireland.

Cover design Michael O'Brien
Cover illustration Keggie Carew
Typesetting by Photo-Set Ltd.

1

The moment of consecration approached. There was much clearing of throats, something which irritated him greatly, something he found almost intolerable. He recognised Mrs O'Callaghan's cough and knew it accurately identified her as an imperious person. He picked out the nervous bray of Mr O'Sullivan, the retired school teacher, not long a widower; and the loud, assertive hawk of Mrs Kinnane, a woman he thought boisterous and opinionated and, despite all her material possessions, forever marked by mind, manner and speech as one of the lower orders and treated as such by the town. He identified also, the repetitive rasp of Mrs Grogan; an image of her harassed face presented itself sharply. Her hair prematurely grey and lacklustre. Her face thin and pinched, particularly about the mouth. Her eyes had a numb, animal-like deadness which clearly identified her as a victim of her husband's brutality during his frequent bouts of drunkenness.

He coughed dryly and sought to dismiss all thoughts of worldly things. He intoned the prayer as prescribed by ritual. "Hoc est enim Corpus meum." He genuflected and the server struck the sanctuary bell three times. Rising, for some seconds he held up the consecrated host for public worship and out of habit found himself repeating the childhood prayer he had been taught, "My Lord and my God". He placed it on the silver paten and joined together his fingers and thumb. He took the chalice and proceeded to the consecration of the wine. He genuflected, prayed and, rising, elevated the cup. Briefly he held it aloft and then positioned it safely on the altar. The sanctuary bell rang again three times and echoed strongly for some seconds high up about the stained rafters. As if on a given signal the small congregation broke into coughs and sighs and, again, much clearing of throat.

His mouth was dry and foul. He refrained from intoning, as he had for so many years, the prayers of adoration and gratitude at the bread made flesh, the wine made blood. His hands trembled.

Darkness threatened. He grasped the edge of the altar, telling himself that, as in the past, the spell would pass and he would soon recover. Mr Whelan, whose presence at daily mass was as spasmodic as his drinking, blew his nose fastidiously into a fresh handkerchief. He trumpeted rather than blew, something the priest found unpleasant. He knew all the people from their churchly eccentricities but could hardly recognise them on the street. Mr Duran, his sacristan and server, rose and glided to the marble altar rails which divided the sanctuary from the church proper and with the expertise of years of service flicked the altar cloth up over the balustrade. Genuflecting before the high altar, he crossed over to gospel side and repeated his action.

The more assured members of the congregation left their seats in the body of the church and, approaching the rail, knelt, their heads bowed. He silently recited the post-communion prayers. They were punctuated by the booted arrogance of Mr Swinton-Devett, one of a catholic family which had held property for many generations in what was primarily a protestant garrison town, who made his way to the altar as though bestowing his presence as a privilege to all gathered there.

He took communion under both species. As he broke and swallowed the host deep disgust arose within him. His lips moved as though in prayer. He received the wine and again pretended devotion. As always an image of his mother crossed his mind. Vague. Veiled. Harrowed beyond bearing, grieving ceaselessly for John. He prayed, "May perpetual light shine upon her, may she rest in peace." Loving memory rather than religious belief prompted him. There had been little he could do to appease the suffering of her last years on earth and now it was he rather than she who desperately needed peace.

He genuflected and took the ciborium from the tabernacle. Lifting the rather heavy vessel in his hands, he took out a host between the thumb and forefinger of his right hand and turning to the congregation he held it up and intoned: "Ecce Agnus Dei, ecce qui tollis peccata mundi." He then recited the 'Domine non sum Dignus' three times and descended to the rails to distribute the communion. He found himself confronted by many heads bowed before the exposed host and he felt anew a simple gratitude for those whose faith and fervour was sufficiently strong to have them rise from their beds and travel, in some instances considerable distances on foot and most, if not all, fasting. Warmth surged through him. He experienced something akin to love for his flock whom he often thought of as shittened sheep, and he, their shittened shepherd. He steadied himself against the fetid draught of breath which would break over him as he distributed the communion, laying each wafer carefully on the distended tongues of the parishioners. He was determined, if at all possible, not to physically touch them at their most objectionable: furred tongues protruding, mouths agape, rotten and scaled teeth and, in the cases of the poor and the elderly, toothless, shrunken gums. Hardly had he commenced when nausea overcame him. He stumbled slightly and Mr Duran, who was about to precede him with a silver salver to place under the chins of those receiving, reached up and caught him firmly by the arm.

He snorted in anger and went rigid with shock. He shook himself free of the man's grasp. Mr Duran paled and for the rest of the time it took to complete the distribution the server kept his head bowed, his face and even the tips of his big, hair-tufted ears red with embarrassment. The rest of the mass passed without incident. He finished and imparted the final blessing. He divested in the sacristy and prayed for some minutes. Then he roundly rebuked Duran for catching his arm during communion, an impertience and violation of his person. He cut short the old man's apologies and self-justification. Father Phelan entered the sacristy to vest for the last mass of the day just as he had finished his diatribe. He greeted them both with characteristic warmth: "Good morning again, Canon. Good morning, John." He glanced sharply at them, sensing the tension and realising that there had been a sharp exchange of words. Mr Duran replied heartily and with pleasure. The Canon contented himself with a mere nod of the head in the general direction of the fat priest, a reformed alcoholic and womaniser who had been removed from his previous position because of his scandalous conduct. But he was by far the most popular cleric in the parish, particularly in the poorer districts.

He took his leave as quickly as possible without farewell and, crunching across the gravel laid all round the church, he passed through the gate in the high wall and entered the grounds of the Parochial House. It was a morning of sharp, perfect light and early summer flowers were already in bloom. He was scarcely aware. His hands still pained from the chilblains which afflicted him every winter and took a considerable time to clear up. He passed down the path which led to the house and, skirting the building, made for the garden proper, his fury at Duran's behaviour still unabated. His mass had been superficial mummery and its celebration brought him neither strength nor comfort. In his better moments he did concede that what to him was empty ritual performed out of a simple resolution to discharge his duties as the senior priest of his parish, was of deep significance to his congregation. He had seen Mrs O'Sullivan watching from his bedroom window. She would keep breakfast hot until Father Phelan could join them. She feared him, he knew, and perversely it afforded him a grim pleasure. One he knew to be despicable, but pleasing.

The garden at first glance had an air of abandonment but in time one recognised the signs of care lavished on it by Guard Mullins, who attended to the flower beds and the few apple trees they somewhat grandly called the orchard in return for the use of a sizeable plot to the south of the house which would have otherwise lain fallow. The Canon had agreed to the arrangement less out of any advantage to himself — he had no great dislike of wild gardens, in fact they pleased him by their vigour and the resilience which survived slow strangulation by grass and undergrowth — but because the guard was from one of the south-eastern counties and was struggling to educate and care for his young family of three, their mother having died in childbirth. In the plot allocated to him he grew potatoes and vegetables of all kinds which he supplied to the two hotels in town. In addition he supplied the same together with fruits and even honey to the Parochial House, which was already well supplied by the neighbouring farmers. He respected Mullins because he was a taciturn man who rarely spoke, other than to offer a polite greeting or comment on the state of the weather and the progress of the war in Europe. He was disliked in the town because, though diligent in his duties, he sometimes hounded people over trivial offences, prosecuting where prudence would dictate a stern warning. He liked to come on his afternoons, days and evenings off and pace the paths, smoking his pipe contemplatively, inspecting the results of his labour at various stages of growth. He was a lonely man who spent a great deal of his time at Our Lady's Shrine in the church. He did not drink, nor did he mix freely with company in the town. He was ridiculed to some extent for devotion to his family, all of whom showed scholastic promise. Nevertheless, the Canon was relieved the guard was nowhere to be seen. He was probably on night duty.

He extracted his breviary from the deep pocket of his three-quarter-length coat and walked the path. The cinders crunched underfoot in what he considered a companionable, comforting manner. 'Marino', the house in which he had been born, had had such a path in the garden and he found some peace by seemly pacing to and fro, praying or simply musing. Usually the crackles beneath his feet evoked some childhood incident or a sequence of pictorial images which solidified into one long-forgotten memory but none presented themselves today. He commenced *The Divine Office*. He loved it greatly though it held nothing but the remnants of a once intense belief in Christ and was his bond to Him as present in the tabernacle or in the consecrated bread and wine of the mass. Loss of belief in all he had held most precious in life had once harrowed him but time and resolution had anaesthetised the pain. He considered the Office and his work as a testament to those who sought hope and strived for betterment. The creation of optimism where it had perished, was not to him an ignoble goal. In certain cases, he knew from the confessional, it gave strength to those who might otherwise be lost, who in failing blight the lives of others. This he thought of as his essential mission in life. Service to those who might otherwise despair. For this he was prepared to continue wearing the cloth. For this obedience to his vows was worthwhile. For this he lived and expected no return here or hereafter.

He paused beside the Lourdes grotto erected by one of his predecessors. It bore a plaque prominently displayed and inscribed with the man's name and the date on which his devotion had been made concrete and visible. He scowled in distaste at the white-clothed figure of the Virgin, with her bland, sanctimonious face, and the kneeling figure of Bernadette staring in doltish devotion at her. The paint was peeling in patches from both statues. It gave them the appearance of lepers but in this instance the flesh-devouring disease extended its insatiable hunger even to the clothing. With a war in progress in Europe and state of emergency in Ireland, there was no hope of summoning workmen from Dublin to restore the figures. That they might pass beyond repair and suffer complete disintegration failed to concern him.

Mrs O'Sullivan appeared at the gate which led directly to the house, shaking her apron as though scattering a number of hens clustering about her. He gestured acknowledgement with a slight wave of the hand. He remembered that he had a sick-call to make later in the morning to a family in Copley's Lane. The thought of being in the same room as a mortally ill person and having to suffer the wretched stench of the sick room effectively killed his appetite, sharpened as it had been by the fine, fresh morning. He turned towards the house, his shadow preceeding him; it aroused the memory of a piece of poetry he had once known. He failed to place it with any certainty and the lapse annoyed him.

Mrs O'Sullivan took his coat and biretta in the hallway. She glanced swiftly at his hands to see if they had healed but refrained from comment, remembering the sharp, snappish retorts she had often received in the past. He folded one mitten in upon the other and carefully placed them in the drawer of the hall-table. "Breakfast is ready, Canon," she said shortly, "any time you are." She made her way to the kitchen at the back of the hall, her walk sounding loudly on the shining linoleum. The polish she used was synthetically scented with lavender, which he had told her he found repugnant. There were however certain areas where Mrs O'Sullivan brooked no trespass. She ruled the house rigidly if passively and had broken the teeth of many a strong cleric since her early widowhood.

Father Phelan was seated at the dining table. He rose to greet his superior as he entered the room and the Canon replied with an irritable flap of his hand as he took his seat at the top of the table. The room was sunny and warm. The older priest slumped against the back of the chair. The sunlight, intensified by the glass of the windows, played pleasantly on his face and hands. He felt a sense of wellbeing he had not experienced for some time. Father Phelan tied his napkin about his neck, instead of placing it across his lap, in the belief that it was the correct thing to do. Example, the Canon reflected, was not as effective as one might like to think. The sight of the curate looking like an obese and unruly child intent on licensed gluttony appealed to his sense of the absurd. They waited. The clock on the mantlepiece ticked away loudly in the silent, sunlit room.

Father Phelan addressed him. He had been fervently hoping he would not. "It's powerful to see the first signs of summer, Canon. Powerful altogether."

He guardedly agreed with a nod of the head. To speak, he felt, would only encourage further conversation. His tactic failed.

"A few more weeks and summer will be wild altogether!" There was something of the infectious good humour of a schoolboy about enthusiasm, but he had no wish to breakfast with a schoolboy. The curate paused and then plunged ahead, his face a mask of innocence. "Tell me, do you believe in this theory that the seasons are changing, or to be more precise, the climate is changing? They say for instance, we are not getting the summers we used to get in the old days."

The Canon looked at the man, seeking the slightest indication that he was being frivolous at his expense. He saw nothing but bland good fellowship. "I fail to see how I can be expected to confirm or refute the assertion, Father."

"Well now, I'll put it more bluntly. Were the summers in your day, your youth, any better than they are now?"

The older priest hesitated. "Not noticeably I should say." As he had hoped, Father Phelan lapsed into silence.

Mrs O'Sullivan entered the room and lay their plates of porridge before them. Father Phelan added country butter and a liberal sprinkling of salt. He contented himself with a little sugar. He hoped the arrival of the food would silence his breakfast companion but eating, he had noticed, opened Father Phelan's mouth in more respects than one.

"Good news on the wireless this morning, Canon?

He had as usual listened to an early morning BBC broadcast for information on the progress of the war. "Yes. Or what I would consider good news. There are, I know, some who might not agree with me. The Germans are hard-pressed, everywhere they are not quite living up to their reputation." He glanced briefly at the curate from under his eyelids to see if his remarks had in any way affected him. But his assistant contented himself with a fatalistic shrug of his shoulders. A passionate nationalist, Father Phelan had been much in demand for republican funerals in the past and still took the annual prayers of remembrance at the graves of some of the town's notable leaders who had died in the fight for independence. The man had come to his parish with a greater reputation for political sympathies than for his sanctity or devotion to priestly duty.

"You have to see the Madden girl — God help her — this morning, Canon. I'll take the call if you like."

The comment was lightly and, superficially at least, politely made. Nevertheless it both shocked and enraged him, all the more because when people came to summon a priest to the death-bed of a relative in most cases they asked specifically for Father Phelan. Father Good, he knew, came second and he trailed very badly in third place. Yet while it was true that he loathed sickness and human infirmity in general, he had at one time loved the 'sick call'. He loved the mission of bringing to the bedside of the dying, the Holy Viaticum, the food for a journey. In many respects he had considered it the greatest of his privileges. He had often felt then — as he had when distributing communion to young children for the first time in their lives — that he was close to the seat of his priestly power and that great graces flowed to the sick, the afflicted, the very innocent and the very old, through his most unworthy hands. Now he no longer believed this, yet it was of paramount spiritual importance to him that the ritual gave relief to those who might otherwise suffer considerable distress and fear. His disbelief did not wholly impair his effectiveness and with the ill, the troubled, the bereaved, he felt something akin to compassion assert itself within. Such depths of emotion were alien to his personality and he felt they might overcome him unless ruthlessly kept in control.

He glared at Father Phelan in detestation. "That's very kind of you, Father. You think, perhaps, I am incapable of discharging my duties?"

The cold venom of his words struck the curate with force. The smile vanished from his face, his mouth quivered, his hands and his voice shook. He stammered when he spoke. "Why no, Canon. Of course not!" He had the advantage. Impelled by capricious cruelty he sought to hurt if not to wound the man by his side. A man, he knew quite well, who had not wholly escaped pain and affliction. The knowledge did nothing to moderate his spleen. "Then perhaps you think I am an unfit person for my position as parish priest of this parish?"

The question hung suspended in the sunlit morning air. The doorbell rang as if from a great distance down a long corridor of silence. Mrs O'Sullivan's heavy tread sounded on the linoleum. They heard her open the door and welcome Father Good, who returned her greeting as he did all other things: with excessive gentleness. Their voices penetrated the dining room but did nothing to disperse the heightened tension.

From the walls canons in clerical robes, badly painted without exception, gazed down upon the scene from within guady, tarnished gilt frames. The eyes of these, and others in photographic portraits of the more recent past, mirrored one truth — or so he always thought — the sorrowful realisation of the mutability of all things. Whatever the cause, their sharp eyes betrayed a startling vulnerability.

Father Phelan with one hand shaded his right eye as his eyelid twitched rapidly. He waved his left hand in a gesture of despair. "No, Canon. Of course not. The thought had never occurred to me."

The loathing churned about inside him. He recognised it as self-hatred and suddenly his anger abated. He spoke but his voice was cold and measured, and though correct, without warmth. He knew it to be so but could not affect what he did not feel. "I believe you, Father. Forgive me. I was unjust."

He turned aside from the man he had deliberately humiliated. He gazed through the window at the garden outside. On the pathway a thrush with a snail in its beak tried to break the shell by tapping it against the cinders. It failed to do so. Perplexed, it dropped the shell momentarily and its head swung from side to side as though seeking something. It picked up the snail in its beak once more and hopped to a stone edging the path. The bird pounded the snail against it. The shell fragmented. Then the bird feasted avariciously on the soft flesh within.

The air was mellow with a pale, golden light, reminding him of the holidays abroad in his youth, characteristic of Northern Italy, Venice in particular in April or early May before the sun was harsh and distorting. He saw his mother in willowly white dress with a hat of transparent material, a bunch of delicate but artificial violets tucked into the pearl grey band. His father was there, in light summer clothing and quite unsure whether he should relax and enjoy himself; a man who rarely allowed himself a foreign tour, preferring instead a solitary sojourn in the west of Ireland where he could make a respectable pretence at being a competent fisherman. John must still have been alive then though the Canon had no memory of him being with them on their visit to Venice. His mother's laugh was light and silvery when the bells of Saint Mark's rang out and the squat over-fed pigeons took flight and wheeled across the shimmering city of dark, clean waters; a city which was to impress itself upon his mind as a mixture of the miraculous, the beautiful and the squalid. Yes, John must have been alive then and with them. Otherwise his mother would never have laughed so lightly nor worn white. He took out a handkerchief. Emotion surged inside him. He tried urgently to hide it. Excusing himself, he blew his nose loudly, distractingly, as Mrs O'Sullivan entered with their breakfast on a tray.

Father Good trailed behind her and greeted them with deference. He took a seat at the table at a nod from the Canon. Mrs O'Sullivan laid their plates beside them and placed the teapot within easy reach of Father Phelan who had turned to Father Good and was grinning good naturedly.

"Well, boy, they let you out without tearing you limb from limb. They must like you, boy, they must like you! Either that or they're fattening you up for Reverend Mother's feast day!"

'They' were the nuns in the convent where Father Good had said the morning mass. The new arrival flushed a deep red. His eyes sparkled with delight whenever Father Phelan teased with him but usually he avoided looking at anyone directly. He was a taut, nervous man in his mid-twenties and though not effeminate, his sexuality appeared to lack clarity. This the Canon felt was something the young man was going to have to face sooner or later unless by happy chance he forever remained innocent. The Canon had long ago noticed that his presence induced an almost unbearable tension in the young priest. He invariably stammered, which he did not do normally. His colour heightened and his hands which were long and slender became an encumberance rather than the natural extension of his upper limbs. With infinite patience and tenderness he instructed the altar boys in Latin, to instil in their uncaring minds the stately language of the universal church; the elaborate rituals of the mass, both high and low; and the complex, lovely ceremonies of Holy Week which usually defeated the most devoted teachers. He did not altogether labour in vain though the Canon preferred to be served at mass by Duran rather than by a boy, half asleep and liable to trip while transferring the missal from one side of the altar to the other.

Father Phelan had taken to him on sight and the friendship of the stout, extrovert man of undoubted masculinity was something Father Good cherished and relied upon to an extent neither fully realised. The senior curate believed the friendship made possible the younger man's work and that if he was ever deprived of that support he might falter and fail. For his part, the Canon's feelings towards the young priest were a compound of lukewarm pity and contempt for someone who depended so desperately on evoking a favourable response in those to whom he ministered. Popularity was more than suspect: it was deplorable.

The parish priest examined whether or not he should reprimand Father Phelan for his irreverent reference to the nuns but decided to accept it as intended, lightly and in fun, a device to allow Father Good to join the company without embarrassment. Besides, he reminded himself, thanks largely to the young man's prosperous merchant family the Parochial House was assured of more than its fair share of rationed food and other generous allowances which made possible many gifts to the poor of the parish. These Father Good delivered with open-handedness though not always wisely.

The distribution of charity was something the Canon despised, considering it a contemptible effort to purchase the affection and spiritual loyalty of those incapable of exercising necessary discipline in their lives. This failure, together with a tendency to drunkenness, was in his opinion the fundamental cause of poverty. Charity as thus understood demeaned everyone, demeaned none so much as the giver. The poor, he had quickly discovered in the first years of his own ministry in the most poverty stricken areas of the city, loathed the giver with a racial hatred which was hideously intense. Brutality both mental and physical they could forgive, but kindness they never forgave.

Nothing demonstrated the fact so well as that silver pin-point of malice which shone in their eyes as they mouthed false, if profuse, gratitude.

Father Phelan poured a cup of tea for the young priest and passed it to him. Father Good accepted and expressed his thanks. Carefully he measured less than the allocated amount of sugar per person as laid down by the laws governing rationing. He seemed to consider it a heroic act of self-sacrifice and to believe that the mind of God was moved by such matters. Silence descended.

"Fancy a round of golf, boy?" Father Phelan's voice was less jovial now. There was a distinct element of the defiant in it. Father Good, swallowing with difficult, darted a glance in the parish priest's direction at the head of the table. "If the Canon has no objections," he managed without too much stuttering.

The Canon glanced at them both contemptuously, wondering how such a nondescript person as Father Phelan could arouse such hatred in him. He considered himself above all a controlled, self-possessed person not without some detachment; nevertheless he found himself clenching his teeth and tightening his fists to the point where his hands hurt. "No," he snapped shortly, the venom in his voice astonishing even himself. "I have no objection whatever." Abruptly he rose, crumpled his napkin into a ball and flung it onto the table. He stalked from the room, slamming the door behind him.

He sought the refuge of his own room and sank into the ungainly armchair, one of a pair flanking the open fireplace in which a bunch of honesty sprouted from a jam-crock wrapped in red crêpe paper. A fire was rarely if ever lit there. A one-bar electric fire sufficed. Even that was subject to regular power cuts and could not be depended upon for heat. The room faced south and was sparsely furnished. In the niche opposite the further window stood his bed, one of the kind described as an army 'cot' and often seen in the poorer homes in the town. By it, a small bedside table on which stood a rarely needed alarm clock. He woke unfailingly each morning at six o'clock and had done so since his early childhood. A reading lamp, an open packet of antiseptic throat lozenges and a selection from his large collection of paperback detective stories, mostly published by Penguin, completed his needs. In a nearby bookcase sat works of a more devotional kind published during the last century, bound in leather with gold lettering now somewhat faded; untouched they had remained since the day some thirty years ago when on first seeing them he examined them out of curiosity and, replacing them, wondered at the dead disputations of that century much given to theological debate conducted in limpid prose and unbridled savagery. To the right of the shelves hung an uninspiring crucifix, larger than the ordinary, its slung body of Christ, so white and unlovely, never failing to remind him of the slimy underbellies of the slugs, for whom Mullins laid poison in the garden, those he squeezed remorsely to death between his thumb and forefinger. The five wounds of the crucified Christ were visible and from them flowed an excess of blood, once garishly scarlet but now turned brown from exposure to sunlight. Below the crucifix and positioned some feet from the wall was a *prie-dieu*. Here he had once entered into his private devotions, in the past apt to be both prolonged and intense. Between the two windows of the room stood a beautifully polished wash-stand of the kind fashionable in his childhood. Its top was of veined marble and on it stood a handsome porcelain pitcher and bowl which he used daily to wash, preferring the privacy of his room rather than the bathroom. Above the stand hung a shaving mirror and, on the wall by it, a small shelf on which were laid out with obsessive neatness: a stick of shaving soap, now not readily available in the chemist shops; his sable shaving brush; toothpaste and toothbrush; an open razor; and a tube of some sticky antiseptic substance — which operated on the same principle of a tube of ladies lipstick — he used to staunch the blood should he cut himself while shaving. A large wardrobe dominated the wall opposite. The room could be said to be almost spartan and revealed nothing of the mind of the man who lived there. Which was precisely as he wished it to be.

Pain, short and stabbing, shot across his forehead. He put the arched fingers of his right hand to his temples and pressed as tightly as he could in an effort to ease the pain. He failed. It increased rather than lessened and his breathing became steadily more laboured. His mouth fell open and hung slackly. Saliva accumulated behind his teeth and very quckly dribbled from his lips. He was about to lose consciousness when he heard a short tap on the door. Mrs O'Sullivan, thinking the room unoccupied, entered carrying a change of bed linen. She froze. "Are you alright, Canon?" she asked anxiously.

His face seemed paralysed. He tried to gain her attention by rolling his eyes. Distraught, Mrs O'Sullivan wiped her hands frantically on her white apron. "I had better get Father Phelan," she muttered aloud on the edge of panic. He reacted violenty and gathering all his will he managed a strangulated "No!" She stared at him, uncertain. "Very well, Canon," she said. "If you wish, so." Doubtfully she came towards him and, kneeling, gently dabbed at his dribbling mouth with her handkerchief. She placed her hand on his forehead. It was deathly cold. "I'll give your face a wash, Canon. Maybe it will help." Unable to oppose her he sank back against the headrest of the armchair and waited dejectedly for her return. She came back quickly with a basin of tepid water, a towel and a sponge. She wiped his mouth free of mucus and patted his forehead with the dampened sponge. She then cleaned his stained soutane. Vigorously she wiped his face and then dried it. Somewhat refreshed though not greatly relieved, he hid his head, weary and defeated.

From a distance he heard the sharp, joyous bark of a dog. Mrs O'Sullivan clicked her tongue in disapproval. The hearty voice of his assistant rang through the house, "Jump, boy, jump!" and to the clicking of his fingers the Canon's splendid Irish setter leaped and bounded into the air, barking delightedly. He resented momentarily, as he always did, Father Phelan's familiarity with Bran but was appeased by the belief that the dog's final loyalty was to him, the master. "Off boy, off!" shouted Father Phelan. With a high yelp the setter bounded up the staircase and within a few seconds was pawing frantically at the door. Mrs O'Sullivan, resigned to mutilated doors, let him in. Bran leaped to the figure slumped in the armchair.

He extended a hand which the dog licked affectionately and then, feeling it must seem repulsive to an onlooker, he hastily withdrew it. "I'll get you a cup of tea, Canon," the housekeeper said, less panic-stricken now. "It might do you some good." He struggled a little and found he had recovered his speech. "That would be very welcome, Mrs O'Sullivan," he said, adding as she went, "I forbid, I absolutely forbid you to discuss with the others what you have just seen." His tone was brutal, commanding submission. "Yes, Canon," she said tightly, her voice jammed with bitterness. "I understand," and flushing with indignation that he should consider any such caution was necessary, she left the room. Silence enveloped the house. Bran had settled by his chair. Blindly the Canon groped for his head and stroked it absentmindedly. The dog licked his hand and this affection pleased the priest.

2

The parish priest entered the church and quietly approached the high altar. He could see no one in the silent interior. In the side aisles, pools of diffused colours — reds, blues, and ambers — lay beneath the stained-glass, the windows themselves fleetingly visible as first conceived by the artist in that one bright moment of inspiration when he had first visualised them as a vibrant totality, the ideal mixture of prepared material and chance sunlight. Suspended above the sanctuary was the silver plated lamp, the crimson light in its container of tinted glass shedding its brightness everywhere; evoking brief memories of his childhood, the nightlight in his room, the scant homes of the poor with their votive lamps before the shrine of the Sacred Heart.

He genuflected and took the ciborium of consecrated hosts from inside the tabernacle, feeling that he was rifling the tomb of one once so alive and much beloved. The wafer, he reminded himself, had no intrinsic value. The faith, and the only the faith of the poor, the deprived, the devout, gave it whatever value it might be said to possess. He genuflected again and took out from the inside pocket of his greatcoat, the silver pyx wrapped in linen. He lay the host in the pyx and wrapping it carefully returned it to his pocket. He prayed or rather hoped, and both he knew for him were inextricably interwoven, that the white bread which he was to transport on his person across the town to the waiting communicant might in some way alter the irreversible progress of the disease which would in its last stages subject its victim to indescribable pain. Pain which could not be effectively alleviated by the use of drugs which were in peacetime imported from the belligerent countries and who were now retaining them for the use of their own people and had little to spare for a country they considered hostilely neutral.

The recipient of the host would be a young girl in her early twenties, of good background though her family was now living in somewhat straightened circumstances. She was not, he remembered, strikingly beautiful and her devotion had never been above that expected from a girl educated in the local convent school, yet he was expectant as he had never been before when setting out on similar visitations in the past. He made his way from the sanctuary and down the aisle.

At the end of the church, kneeling in the shadows, was a woman lost in private devotion. Her shoulders were swathed in a silver fox-fur even on so warm a day, her face hidden by the wide brim of an unfashionable hat and its hanging veil of flecked net. He immediately recognised her as the wife of a small publican who had established himself as a timber merchant before the war broke out; he had grown wealthy on the insatiable need for timber — created by the shortage of coal — that had stripped the land of trees. An unhappy woman, a stranger from some remote part of the country, she had never gained the acceptance she sought from those who considered themselves her social superiors. Childless, her marriage was unhappy. She was lonely and suffered accordingly. She lifted her head and turned her troubled eyes towards him. He touched his breast with the palm of his right hand to indicate he was carrying the sacrament. She blessed herself and returned to her prayers.

He emerged into the strong sunlight of the sunny morning. Bran was waiting in anticipation of his morning walk. He thrashed his tail about and gazed devotedly at the Canon. "Stay," he commanded. The dog sprawled submissively on the gravel, whining and still thrashing his tail.

Stepping over the animal, he paused at the head of the steps which fell in varying levels to streets below the high hill on which the church was built; he gazed for some seconds at the long, cemented facade of the convent situated on a hill opposite, barely visible behind its high walls and screen of sheltering trees now beginning to bud. As always, he raised his biretta to the convent as a mark of respect to the women within who, whilst educating the young girls of the town's better families, were also engaged in what he saw as a heroic struggle for sanctity in the midst of entrenched mediocrity. Oddly, he thought, I do not believe in the Godhead, yet I believe in sanctity. Its strange supernatural force he could only describe as grace.

He descended to the street below. Most people would content themselves usually with a mere nod of the head in greeting. Very few men would salute. Very few would smile openly or generously. Some would studiously ignore him or in a few instances would seek to meet his eye only to register unmistakable hostility. Now with his right hand held to his left breast and unaccompanied by his dog, they realised that he was bearing the host and blessed themselves hurriedly or averted their gaze altogether.

Having come down Church Steet he turned into South Main Street and paused to study its rather narrow length, now without motor traffic of any kind. In the years before the war it had been a bustling, prosperous town, the finest trading centre in the western half of the county. Today only one or two horses and carts were tethered outside shops or stores and the view could be seen to better advantage. The houses were of uniform height and built about the same time, perhaps as long as two hundred years ago. They had a linear beauty devoid of all unnecessary embellishment, the product of the planter protestants who had founded the town and had maintained it as a fortress in a province staunchly catholic by tradition. They — the planters — exhibited, as he frequently had to admit, exceptionally good taste, a fine feeling for public buildings and private dwellings which blended harmoniously with the landscape.

His progress was rapid, unimpeded in any way. He crossed the stout bridge spanning the broad river which gave the town its name. A soft, cool breeze blew upstream, quite unlike the whipping wind which prevailed for most of the year. He crossed the small triangle by the Bank and the former Orange Hall, now less provocatively named, and made his way down Mill Street. He drew a deep breath and held it for as long as he possibly could, knowing that sooner or later the stench of poverty and its accompanying odours of demoralisation and desperation would soon assail him from all sides. With it would come the pungent smell of human excrement from the open sewers of the hovels in Langly Square and Begley's Lane, and to him the particularly revolting tang of unwashed bodies and unclean abodes.

The first few houses on the right hand side of the street — those backing onto the river — were solid examples of eighteenth and early nineteenth-century Irish provincial architecture. Four storeys high, green-slated with delineated facades, they possessed well spaced, high windows, handsome portals of stone and doors of the stoutest timbers painted in most cases a dull green and in one instance stark, uncompromising black. Above the doors were delicate fanlights and each had a fine flight of steps to the front door. They were without exception the residences of respectable and valued members of the community. One or two protestant families lived in accord though not familiarity with their catholic neighbours. The loyalties of the householders could be judged on the death of a pope or an English monarch. For the burial of a pope only the catholics pulled down the window blinds and draped the brass knockers on the front door in black crêpe. When Queen Victoria and later Edward died practically all the houses had their blinds lowered. Here too as nowhere else in town they strew straw before the houses of those mortally ill. They represented for him all that was best in the growing middle-class which was beginning to flower under British rule when nationalism and the more insidious doctrines of Marxism had asserted themselves. The standards of decent and fair behaviour which were valued attributes of the protestant ascendancy had terminated in the petty but savage disputations of Irish republicanism. From that debility sprang the more dreaded doctrines of socialism and the manifestly absurd belief in the equality of men. He regretted the departure of the British garrison some twenty years previously, as did the occupants of those imposing houses. It had resulted in the isolation of Ireland and deprived it of the possibility of becoming the motherland of a spiritual empire, it inflicted the lacerating effects of a militant nationalism whose ideological disputes rivalled in intensity and surpassed in hatred those of the early church. He sighed deeply, unaware that he was so doing.

He suddenly found himself passing the abandoned hulk of the old co-operative creamery, which was made of galvanised iron sheeting. In disuse it had rusted, the windows had been broken and it was decrepit in the extreme. He never passed the place without thinking it should be razed to the ground without further thought. It was, he knew through the confessional, a place widely favoured for illicit sexual assignations and the haunt of vandals and layabouts. About it the wasteland was thickly covered with weeds of all kinds. Dock, thistle, ragwort, sorrel and sedges flourished there in abundance. To his left the houses deteriorated and the further he progressed down the street the more decrepit they became. Low set, though slated and two-storied, they soon gave way to mean, squat hovels with plastered and whitewashed earthen walls. At one time the floors of the dwellings had been simple, impacted earth and the roofs thatched with reeds, the thatching now rotten and neglected on all but a few cottages.

During the troubled times they had been burned, their mud walls alone left standing by a southern English regiment in reprisal for an ambush in which some five soldiers perished in the north of the county. The people in the sordid huts had been guiltless but rather than destroy the houses of the upper class, their commanding officer permitted them to rampage through the hovels of the destitute. The occupants had suffered much, though they had lost only such furnishing as was fit for firewood and had benefitted from funds raised to aid them in their distress; the money had come largely from abroad, Americans subscribing with special generosity. The houses were restored, they were re-roofed with sheets of iron and their earthen floors cemented. They also received directly a sizeable sum in compensation, for their discomfort. All in all, he thought surlily, they had received an uncommonly good bargain. The money needlessly to say, had been squandered in a matter of months.

Some grubby children approached in filthy clothing, some barefoot, one or two in boots too big for them and without shoelaces. Their heads were without exception shaven. They looked pallid and ill and many were scabbed about the mouth. They were also plainly scarred by their inadequate diet which he knew in most cases consisted of bread and tea, some few potatoes and rarely if ever, meat. One young girl had an ugly, spreading crater of ringworm set like the mark of Cain upon the centre of her broad forehead. Another had an eye discharging freely and almost closed by the encrustation around it. He recoiled as they approached, addressing him in broad and largely unintelligible dialect; in an excess of devotion they clasped their hands together, genuflected and then blessed themselves with broad self-conscious movements of their right hands. Their eyes were bright and they seemed spirited, at least momentarily, and were not entirely without the fresh beauty and essential virtue of the very young, though he knew their capacity for foul mouthedness and thievery. They had a native wit and sly calculation far above those of their age from more prosperous homes. How long, he wondered, would they retain their innocence in the face of parental brutality, drunkeness, aggression and infidelity. Here, he thought grimly, the young bloods of the town came in search of easy conquest and thoughtlessly destroyed young women, further degrading them in the eyes of all. Here and there in the squalor were a few families whose heroic devotion to their children and their welfare, and to their Holy Mother, the church, shone through the obscene dim like a bright, brave beacon. Their houses were clean, the mothers loving and self-sacrificing and the fathers sober and diligent. All of which made them victims of the foul humour and derision of the lesser ones about them. Here could be seen in the twin banes of the native Irish, racial memory and a propensity for alcohol. He nodded coldly and dis-couragingly at the children, their hands outstretched for small coins.

One boy, more defiant than the rest, stepped boldly forward, stood in front of him and held out his hand, his eyes gleaming with threat. He touched his breast to signal that he was carrying the sacrament but it was too much to expect that they should understand the significance of the gesture. "A tanner," the boy demanded harshly as the other children crowded around in fearful delight at the audacity of one of their number. "Leave me pass," the priest snapped roughly, suppressing the urge to strike the impertinent youth. "A tanner," the boy again demanded and balled his fist as if about to strike out. The Canon punched him even before he was conscious of any movement on his part. The force of the blow sent the boy reeling. He glanced off the uneven wall of a nearby house and cried out in pain. He put his hand to his head and moments later withdrew it. It was stained crimson and blood flowed freely from a long gash across the side of his head. "You fucking cunt," he swore in rage. "You lousy fucking cunt!" Eyes full of hatred he spat directly into the Canon's face. The priest shrank back in horror as the boy lashed out with his foot. The other children scattered, some shocked, some squealing in delight. "How dare you," he raged, "how dare you profane the Lord's annointed!"

A man appeared at the half-door of one of the houses and eyes alight in malicious pleasure, leaned his heavy form on the half-door, watching attentively. A woman, dirty, dispirited if indeed not crushed, ran from another cottage and caught the boy roughly by the hair. "The fucker hit me, Ma, the fucking cunt hit me," he exclaimed, crouching low as if expecting a series of blows. The woman struck him across the mouth and struck him again and again until she shoved him through the doorway and into the kitchen. She turned and nervously wringing her hands she stormed at him with a venemous hiss. "You were very brave, Canon James Fitzgerald! See if you're as brave when I send the boy's father to fucking deal with you. And by God, when he's made shit out of you, I'll set the law on you. I swear by the blood of Christ I will!" She paused and took breath.

He looked at her in dismay. She was about forty, though old for her age, he decided; with her high cheek bones and very fine brown eyes, she had once been beautiful. Her accent was only slight, she enunciated her words perfectly and there was a hauteur about her now that spoke of some breeding and at the least some rudimentary culture. A good woman, he thought disinterestedly, brought low possibly by love of a handsome sot.

The heavy man two or three houses down, cried out in a deep voice. "Aye, do that, Mrs Cronin, Mam. Leave Tom out of it. Send for the Sergeant himself and press charges of assault and battery. That's what it amounts to even under the so called law of this so called Free State of ours, assault and battery. Put him in the dock, Mam, while you have a chance. That's my advice to you". He came from behind the door. He was tall, broad and as strong as the biggest ox. His right foot was in some way maimed, he dragged it slowly behind him. His right hand was mis-shapen and he wore a thin, black leather glove to conceal the deformity.

The priest recognised the man immediately. He was Jack Whelan, a republican with a reputation as a killer and the man believed responsible for the slaying of a policeman on the very threshold of the Church in the unsettled times of the early nineteen-twenties. The constable had been a catholic and was most effective as an intelligence agent, having been in the district for many years he had a remarkable memory for the details of the town dwellers and those from the surrounding county. A native of Donegal, he was considered a renegade even by those who had little republican sentiment. He had been escorted to the church by an armed guard. Someone had shot the guard and then the constable. Whelan was seized in a raid on a farmhouse some miles outside the town. He was taken to the city gaol and though the officials involved, including British Army officers, had denied all claims of torture and ill-treatment, the man had emerged a cripple from his interrogation. Shortly afterwards he had escaped and had relentlessly hunted and slain most of his torturers. He had not accepted the Treaty and had been hunted like a stag until trapped on the mountains, at bay he had taken his stand in a gun-battle with his pursuers, he received a number of serious wounds and against expectation survived and was imprisoned. Eamonn De Valera, President of the Irish Free State council by 1932, had granted him amnesty on the grounds of compassion. A drunkard now, he was frequently to be seen lying helplessly in a gutter of one of the town's streets. Though destructive and, along with many of his compatriots, rarely forgiving, he was intelligent and formidable. Were it not for his fanaticism he could have served with distinction any cause he chose. Extreme and intolerant however, he elected to play the role of a sea-green incorruptible and was duly abandoned, even in time by his most blinkered admirers.

Whelan now inched his way to where the woman stood on the footpath. "Never mind setting your man on him, Mam. That's just what the cur in canonical clothing wants, though God knows, that's what the bastard needs and should get, a thrashing to within an inch of his life. A horsewhipping, or a pistol-whipping if it comes to that. And I swear to God Almighty if I had my health I'd gladly oblige and do the job here and now.

Canon James Fitzgerald," he spat at the dusty gutter, "traitor to his seed, breed and generation like all the Papishers. Go on up to the barracks, Mam, and set Mr Cosgrave's whelps in blue, our so-called Civic Guards, on this fatted mongrel in his pompous finery." He gritted his teeth, baring them like a hungry hound. Hatred oozed from every tissue of the man's being. "I'll sign my name to any statement to the effect that I saw him do the deed, and by Jesus I'll put my hand on any bible and swear it was so, be it the authorised or the Saint Jerome version. I stand by you, Mam. I stand by you through thick and thin. You and yours were good to me and mine in troubled times and I'll not forget that fact until the day I die. This bastard was in and out of Major Filstraw's room above in the army barracks — in the intelligence room giving what aid he could to Ireland's enemies — the same bastard who denied the rites of Christian burial to many a republican and refused them the right to rest by their forefathers in consecrated ground. You go on up to the barracks, Mam. I'll take the child to a doctor and get a signed medical report. There's one or two men in this town who aren't shit-scared of ecclesiastic displeasure."

The woman looked at the Canon and then at Whelan, whose mouth was flecked with foam. She was obviously loath to take his advice outright. "Come in, Jack, and have a look at the boy for me and then we'll see what to do."

"I'll get that man," was the reply. "And more besides if necessary."

He shuffled inside the house, the woman following swiftly and banging the door behind her, top and bottom. He heard the sound of bolts being shot home and the low murmur of voices as if conspiring. He stood, too shocked to move. Mechanically he took a handkerchief from his pocket and wiped the boy's filthy spittle from his face. Bunching it in distaste he slung it from him as unclean. Tainted. Foully so.

Whelan's assertion that the priest had passed information to Major Filstraw was a savage rumour long current in the town and one that had frequently been flung at him. He had reason to visit the barracks both during and after the First War. Sometimes to attend to the spiritual needs of the men imprisoned there and to those of the garrison who were catholic. On many an occasion he had to deal with the affairs of a woman who had lost her husband or son in the war and had also to enquire about those of his parishioners who were seriously wounded. In two cases he had called to write witnessed reports of good character for two young men who had stood court-martial for some offence or other on

the field of battle. He considered the thankless tasks as
confidential, thus laying himself open to charges of collaboration
and treachery. He had never felt compelled to answer those
accusations thrown at him by some drunken lout who sought to
insult or injure him.

He recalled in bitter detail an incident which occurred during
the Civil War. A young republican had been captured at a village
some miles distant. Under torture he had admitted to the death of
some Free State officers. In revenge he had been tethered by the
hands to the back of a lorry by a rope sufficiently long to drag him
behind. The lorry had then driven off over rough mountainous
roads which were little better than ruts strewn with stones. The
boy's head had been breached in the process and his brains
spilled. Those responsible finally left his hacked body on the
roadside outside the cottage where his mother, on inspecting
what she took to be a bundle of bloodied rags, discovered her son.
The Canon had been summoned to give the last rites and had
taken a hackney motor to the scene. His arrival had been greeted
by derision and jeers. The boy had been a republican and
accordingly excommunicated by decree of the Bishop for bearing
arms against the legally established forces of the State. They had
plainly hoped to see Father Horgan, a priest more active than
even Father Phelan and strongly republican in sympathy. Either
would have without qualm of conscience ignored the decree of
excommunication and administered the last rites. He could not.
Would not. It had been his duty to say so, confronted by the
profaned body of the dead boy and the grief-demented mother.
Only the timely arrival of some Civic Guards with batons
dispersed the hostile crowd who were becoming increasingly
vicious with each passing moment. From that day the boy's death
was commemorated by his people and neighbours. They hung a
picture of Our Lady of Perpetual Succour on a rusted field-gate
nearby and tied jam-jars about it which they filled with flowers.
Here singly or in small groups the neighbours and many who
came from other parishes, knelt briefly in prayer. So was the
decree of the Bishop laid low and rendered as foul as dust while
the memory of the dead was honoured and respected. The events
of that day some twenty years before had not been forgotten, still
less forgiven. It had certainly done nothing to advance his
acceptance among those he then considered his people and whose
affection he had once craved above all else, more than the simple
discharge of their spiritual duties. He had sought their liking if
not indeed their love. It had been withheld. A part of him
perished that day, as often happens under such circumstances.

He leaned against the wall of a house fearing a reoccurrence of his black-out earlier in the day. He was trembling violently and felt that he was about to lose control of his senses. His attack on the child had aroused in him the deepest revulsion not because it had been grossly un-Christian, and unpriestly, but because it was in simple human terms, unworthy. He would have dealt swiftly and ruthlessly with one of his priests had they behaved in such an unbecoming manner. And the episode, he realised with dismay, was far from finished. Should Whelan persist it might involve the law and all that then would result.

He turned down Copley's Lane which led directly to the river and was a favourite watering-place for horses. Just down-river from the shallows a deep pool lay cool and undisturbed. The lane was unpaved and the continual spell of good weather had dried the ruts of the carts and the impress left by the horse's hooves, hard and uneven. Over everything lay a fine film of white dust. To his right going down the lane was a high wall which usually denoted a protestant estate, though not in this instance. Behind the wall rose tall, mature trees. Maples and sycamores, he thought, though he had difficulty in recognising all but the common pine and spruce. On the opposite side were bunched a few cottages in a row but even at the most casual of glances they could be seen to be vastly superior to the cabins and hovels he had just passed. Here the dwellings were well cared for. Their walls were washed in white or yellow and less commonly, blue. The doors were painted, as were the half-porches intended to afford a caller some protection from the elements while waiting at the door. Of obvious Victorian origin, they were fanciful and lent the commonplace a deceptive air of the continental and unfamiliar. The windows, all of which had lace curtains drawn across them, were the final evidence that those who lived within were neither lazy or slothful. Most of the houses had a small garden in front and all were hedged with golden privets, well trimmed. Short flights of steps led to wooden gates and cinder paths to the doors. In the fanlights were statues of the Sacred Heart or the Child of Prague. The piety of the householders could hardly be contested.

He entered the garden of number seven which was the last house in the row and nearest the river. He had scarcely knocked when the door was opened. He was greeted by a woman who all but curtseyed as she said, "Good morning, Canon. You're welcome," and reverently blessed herself.

He took off his biretta and handed it to the woman and stepped over the threshold into a neat and orderly kitchen which reflected the domestic qualities respected by the household. They were, he felt, of decent stock, that rare breed who in the face of all odds try to maintain some standards of decency. On the kitchen table stood a lighted candle in an enamel holder. By it stood a metal crucifix. The woman slowly slipped off his greatcoat and he glanced about. The floor was covered in stone slabs of the kind he remembered so well in 'Marino' and the other quite stately houses of his youth. They could also be seen in the homes of well-established farmers and, remarkably, in the council cottages built during the closing years of the last century. He glanced at the mantlepiece above a well-blacked range in which a fire burned even on so warm a day. A picture of the Sacred Heart hung just above it and before it burned a votive lamp. Once the object of his private love and devotion, indeed the focus of his vain efforts to love even in the abstract, the figure of Christ with the exposed radiant heart as depicted in the worst nineteenth-century art, aroused in him now nothing but aversion.

He grimaced and swallowed as if he had a bad taste in his mouth. The woman glanced at him, her face strained, her eyes showing concern. He glanced at a steep, narrow, enclosed staircase which rose from the kitchen to the girl's bedroom above. The woman gestured him forward. Steeling himself and clenching and unclenching his fist in an outward sign of his inner tension, he started to ascend the unyielding staircase. The woman followed behind at a measured distance carrying the lighted candle.

He had expected a small, dark room with the all-pervasive smell of stale vomit and other excretions which he found so repugnant. Instead he was in a sizeable room fully the length and breadth of the house. It was simply appointed. The parents, he surmised, slept in the room behind the downstairs kitchen. There was a large skylight in the roof and sunlight streamed through onto the figure lying in a large double bed towards the back of the room. For one extraordinary moment he imagined himself on the prow of a ship cutting smoothly through white-capped green waters. He felt the thrust of silent, well-oiled engines and dynamos of huge dimensions. He stood still and drew a short, sharp breath. Yes, he assured himself, she was beyond doubt beautiful in the way all the young are beautiful, but not exceptionally beautiful. She was clearly marked for death and was already much ravaged by her fatal disease. She would not, he thought absently, last long and a quick death would be a blessing to her and to her parents. Her eyes were closed, as though she were comatose. As he advanced silently towards the bed she opened her eyes. He was arrested by their deep brown and despite the intensity with which they shone, the suffering they plainly indicated. Her eyelids flicked in recognition. She smiled. Sadly, he thought.

Moved, he greeted her shortly but gently. "Good morning, my child. How are you this fine morning?" Her lips moved though her words were too faint to hear and her eyes softened in welcome. The woman approached from behind and whispered, "She does have difficulty in talking, Canon." Her voice trembled uncertainly. "It's the pain and the drugs." Her voice held the shock of simplicity.

He nodded. The woman placed her lighted candle at the bedside where already before a tall crucifix other candles were burning on an altar. Such singular marks of respect to the host were rare, he thought, even in middle-class households, better furnished and informed on such matters. He glanced at the mother. She was staring at the figure of her daughter, the light of adoration in her eyes. He took the folded stole from his pocket and kissed the cross embroidered in the centre with threads of gold. Sunlight struck the gold and enhanced the purple silk which reminded him of the bright resurrectionary flowers of Easter, purples, whites and yellows — those which he had once venerated as the flowers of Christ-Come-Again. At a signal from him the woman withdrew, her shining patented leather shoes squeaking noisily on the bare boards of the room and on those of the staircase. He draped the stole about his neck and blessing himself took the pyx from his inner pocket. In its linen wrapping he set it on the bedside table among the flickering candles.

Her eyes were closed again. A spasm of pain rippled across her face. Her body shot taut and then shuddered. She bared her teeth in pain and whimpered like an animal in extremity. He waited for some seconds until the spasm had passed before touching her gently on the shoulder and saying quietly, "I am ready to hear your confession my child." He turned aside and his face assumed the rigidity of the mask he habitually assumed when hearing confessions, to protect himself from the naked hurt and want invariably shown by the penitent. Her voice was long and indistinct. He leaned closer in an effort to distinguish the weak, incomprehensible phrases which fell brokenly from her lips between long, heavy silences. It seemed to him in his heightened state of nervousness and sharpened perception that he could hear the steady beat of her stalwart heart, the flow of blood as it coursed through her body.

She was soon finished. Her transgressions were very few and of no great consequence. He instructed her as penance that she pray for him whenever her health permitted. He laid his hand on her shoulder and pronounced the words of absolution, hoping they might afford her some relief of mind and if at all possible, some spiritual joy.

He coughed and as if by pre-arrangement the woman came upstairs and returned to the bedside. Draped about her head was a colourful scarf of hand-painted silk on which was depicted a colourful scene of the hunt. She wore a heavy coat, obviously her Sunday best, and entwined about her joined hands was a rosary beads. He took the host from the pyx and praying he gave it to the girl, who received it with great difficulty. He had to slip a hand quickly behind her back and tilt her body forward. Fortunately she had sufficient strength to prevent her head from lolling about and he placed the wafer on her barely extended tongue. She had difficulty in retracting it. He took a tumbler of water which stood prepared on the table and putting it to her lips, tilted the glass until her mouth and tongue were moist and she could swallow with relative ease. Gently he laid her back on the pillows. It had been incredibly foolish of him to assume that the girl could receive without difficulty. He would on future visits quarter the host to make it easier for her. He was still astonished at the warmth of her body where he had supported her back with the broad of his hand.

The softness of her flesh confounded him. He tried to remember when last he had touched another body, other than very briefly while anointing. In turn he tried to remember when he had been touched in affection by any being. Apart from the memories of childhood love received from his parents, and they were visual images unrelated to feeling, the only instance he could clearly recall was that June day some forty years before when he had been ordained a priest and the Bishop had laid his hands on his bowed head with strength and warmth and feeling.

He now glanced at her face which was pacific, her lips moving in what he assumed were prayers of adoration. He resolved quietly but determinedly to serve her so long as she should live, humbly and to the best of his ability; he hoped that through religious observances, themselves of no great importance, they might become spiritually united; she might attain some relief from her pain and acceptance of her unhappy lot while he might discover, beneath discarded beliefs, new truths hitherto concealed from him. On impulse he again knelt and joined the woman in silent prayer.

The sunlight in the room was warm and brilliant and as always he found it to some extent debilitating. Distantly he could hear the sound of the town as its inhabitants went about their business. With a sharp twinge which accurately located the true position of his heart, he realised that for once in his life he was in the presence of grace. Great grace which defied the narrow constraints of institutionalised religion. A primitive grace such as sustained mankind through millions of years when as little more than primates they stalked the earth in search of food, loved life and dreaded death and darkness, yet endured on the hope of hopes to come. Graceless himself and now soul-sick he grieved, quietly, deeply.

The woman wiped her eyes. She had been weeping without restraint during her prayers. She rose to her feet and wiped the sweat off the brow of the girl now sleeping peacefully, her upper body rising and falling almost imperceptibly as though was cast adrift upon unduland waters. She smoothed down the bedclothes with a deftness which came from experience. Quickly she extinguished the candles on the table in front of her between her wetted forefinger and thumb. She whispered hoarsely to him, "I'll have a cup of tea ready for you, Canon, when you come down," and hurriedly descended to the kitchen below.

He glanced about the room of the young woman whose life would soon be done. Brutally, considering her youth and unfulfilled life. She was, he had no doubt, a virgin and could now never know a man sexually or be seeded and bear fruit. He mourned the deprivation so inflicted upon her. Sexual union would have given her much physical pleasure and spiritual fulfilment while welding her for all time to the chain of life. Instead she would be lopped off like the diseased limb of a tree incapable of bearing fruit.

He examined the room and its contents. It was sparsely but neatly furnished. A dressing-table on which were neatly arranged the few cheap bottles of perfume, soaps and talcum powders which appealed to young women of her age in the first realisation of their femininity and beauty. All bore labels showing cherry blossoms and were he guessed harshly and synthetically scented. On a nearby table which once evidently served as a desk during her years as a student at the convent, stood her schoolbooks and nearby a few paperback copies of what are loosely called romantic novels. He was pleased to see them there; they represented an innocent desire for all that most appealed to girls. That she showed no great discernment in her reading added a poignancy to her state.

His eyes returned to the still sleeping figure on the bed. For the first time he noticed how long and slender were her hands and neck. Her skin, despite her illness, had a bloom and could be described as flawless. An image flitted across his mind, that of a dead bird, and with it came a memory. Many years ago he had been visiting the home of a friend from his days in the diocesan seminary who had been recently bereaved. The parental home was a farm house of well-worked stone and surprisingly for a two storied house, thatched and carefully maintained. It stood on fertile land and oaks had been planted to give shelter as the locality was flat and exposed. He estimated that the trees were at least a century old and he wondered how a catholic family had secured possession of such fine land long before the agitations of the Land League, founded to secure tenure of land for the small farmer had proved successful. It was autumn and he had tried to avoid the bereaved who were still obsessed with the petty details of the life of the deceased which they were dredging up in an almost hysterical effort to etch his memory on their minds lest it fade completely. He discovered the garden which was overgrown and abandoned and offered a peaceful haven.

The air was still, absorbent. The trees were already shedding their leaves but for the moment were perfectly becalmed. Occasionally with a sad, futile sound a leaf fell from high up in the trees and tumbled down through the branches and remaining leaves, to eventually settle silently on the grass below already strewn with leaves. He sat on a white garden seat in need of repair and a coat of paint. He sat, preoccupied, though by nothing in particular. In the distance could be heard irregular discharge of guns as sportsmen stalked their quarry. The call of the woodpigeon, monotonous and tiresome, persisted despite the shots. Suddenly one swooped into view from somewhere to the right of his vision. It cut slantingly and directly before him and would soon be expected to rise and disappear from sight. But it fell to the earth and lay still. With a start he realised the bird had died suddenly in flight. Shocked, he remained still for some time. Then rising slowly he went to where the bundle lay in the grass and taking it up, held it in his hands. Gently he touched its still warm breast and felt for what he knew would not be there, the beat of its heart. He carried the woodpigeon back to his seat and sat there holding it in his hands. He was overwhelmed by desolation at the fragility, the transience of life in all its form but particularly the human. Bonds of blood and friendships seemed set at nought. Shortly afterwards his friend died while in his thirties. Since then there was no one on the face of the earth he could call friend and he could truthfully assert that there was no one who could claim him as a friend. He ceased to encourage even the most casual of companionships and began instead to explore what the Fathers of the Church had termed the interior mansions of the soul. The exercise had ended in sterility, aridity and finally, loss of belief.

From below the mother softly called: "Canon, Canon," as though she thought he was still engaged in prayer and was loath to disturb him. Quietly he wrapped the pyx in its linen cloth and returned it to the inner pocket of his coat. He took the stole from about his neck and carefully folded it and put it in his pocket. Bracing himself for an emotional encounter with the mother, he made his way downstairs.

The woman gestured towards the table where a cup of tea and some biscuits on a plate were laid for him. On a coloured tile stood a pot of tea and nearby a sugar bowl and a small jug of milk. "The cup of tea, Canon and the few biscuits," she hesitantly suggested. "Maybe you'd like some before you go. The tea will refresh you for the long walk back." Hostility against the rather squat and plump woman with her wringing hands and red, swollen eyes welled in him. He felt she had intruded upon his privacy and had in a sense involved him. He regretted bitterly not allowing Father Phelan to take the visit. His instinct was to refuse curtly. He was aware that if he accepted he would be setting a precedent for future visits. Less selfishly he realised that since tea was severely rationed he was depleting the woman's allowance. Suddenly all anger died, leaving him ashamed and repentant. So he assented after a slight hesitation and sat at the table. The woman beamed and watched him add milk to his tea. He sipped it in silence and taking a biscuit, broke it with a solemnity which unconsciously parodied the breaking of the communion bread, and ate it slowly, bit by bit. He felt incapable of speech though he desired to question the woman who was having difficulty in controlling her emotions.

"Is there no hope?" he asked abruptly, his voice striking even himself as harsh and unsympathetic. The woman's eyes filled with tears. She shook her head. "None at all, Canon," she replied, "except God sees fit to spare her for us." A very unlikely eventuality he thought grimly and searched for something to say which might be of comfort to her. He could think of nothing which would not be dishonest and so remained silent, a dry biscuit between his fingers before eating it. The woman turned away, her shoulders heaving. An alarm clock ticked. He found its erratic sound extremely irritating. The subdued noise of the outside world provided a startling contrast to the relative quiet of the kitchen which he shared with the weeping mother, and upstairs, the prone daughter on her deathbed. He longed to flee.

"Is she an only child?" he asked, his voice dispassionate, remote and not supportive. He was helpless to remove that cold edge of steel which alienated people and possibly at times, wounded. "No, Canon," she replied. "There's four brothers over in England at the moment. Four fine, healthy lads, God be good to them. We haven't let them know about Catherine. They have enough to worry about, what with the war and the bombing and besides, what could they do?" He rose abruptly.

"Thank you for your kindness and consideration," he muttered, seeking only to flee the house and its blighted atmosphere. The woman nodded her head pitifully and held his overcoat as he struggled to get it on. Succeeding, he buttoned it firmly. He shivered involuntarily despite the warmth of the day, the kitchen though noticeably cool was by no means cold. Unaware of what she was doing the mother wiped some dandruff off his collar and let her hand rest for a second on the rich pile of the material. She handed him his biretta. Then as he was about to leave in her agony she clutched his hand. "Canon, Canon, what in God's name are we going to do?" Her wail, her sorrow penetrated to his core. She seeks bread of me, he thought, and I can only give her stone. Her distress unnerved him. The warmth of her small, fat hand revolted him as did any contact with the flesh of another. He spoke as he had to speak for many years, falsely though not wholly so. It was the language of their Church which they expected their priests to use, he spoke it therefore not to deceive but to console. "God is good. Put yourself in His hands. His love and compassion are immeasurable. Commend yourself and your daughter to His divine mercy." He loathed that he should have to utter such sentiments but he had chosen to serve and that demanded in some instances duplicity, though not outright deceit. The balance between the two, he felt, lay slightly in his favour. He withdrew his hand with an effort. The woman dried the tears on her face with the back of her hand as she opened the door for him. "Thank you for coming, Canon. Please God you'll come again." The warmth and generosity and the simple sincerity of her statement surprised him. "Pray for her, Canon. Pray for her in the name of God."

He felt he was an empty vessel devoid of all compassion even for the most harrowing of sufferings. He did however nod assent. He would pray for her during his daily mass. He remembered his pledge to the young woman upstairs, his vow to serve her all her days. "I will come again," he said shortly. "I will come whenever you need me, day or night." With the mother's blessings following him he escaped. He felt greatly disturbed and hurriedly made his way back to the Parochial House. There he left his overcoat and biretta and taking his missal he left for the tree-lined walk behind the cemetery, having instructed Mrs O'Sullivan that he was to be disturbed only under the most pressing circumstances. Bran ran before him yelping excitedly but hardly aware of the dog's presence, the priest paced the path between the chestnuts, dappled light dancing on the dusty rutted surface. He was curiously elated, and expectant, but why he did not know nor could he imagine.

3

Rain and wind rattled the window panes of the room. Outside in the streets he had passed through not long before, the adbare people — he had seen some women wearing only skimpy shawls and no footwear of any kind — sought vainly to protect themselves against the savage, wind driven downpour. In the fireplace a handsome fire of logs was burning. Its careering flames were brightly echoed in the highly polished mahogany furnishings which though impressive were not opulent. If anything they hinted at selective austerity but, as well he knew, selective austerity like selective hunger bore little reality to the experience of the inadequately fed, clothed and sheltered.

He had met the bishop on innumerable occasions when as parish priest he played host during the annual visit for confirmation. He had found him undemanding, at times humorous but essentially withdrawn, rebuffing gently any signs of friendship beyond civility and the deference due to his office. He was a man of frugal habit, given to long hours of prayer and meditation. Nothing then could have prepared him for the suffering he saw in the face of the man who rose from behind his desk and came forward to greet him, refusing to extend his ring for the homage which was his right as a spiritual lord. He had aged but was in no way infirm. After the priest had risen from his knee the Bishop warmly shook his hand and gestured towards an armchair, gilded and padded in faded gold plush. Between the chairs was a low table and on it rested an ashtray, a cigarette case and some matches in a silver holder. Behind them was one of the rain-obscured windows, its curtains undrawn. He was grateful he had not been seated directly in front of the fire. Intense heat like undue cold he found distressing. The bishop waited for him to sit before taking his place in the chair opposite and after greeting him warmly again and enquiring about the health of his priests and housekeeper, wisely allowed the conversation to lapse. Some twenty odd years had passed since that silence fell, but pacing the path beneath the trees he could still remember it. Rain tatted at the window panes setting them awash, distorting the night view of the city deep in the valley below.

Quietly, unemotionally, he laid his problem before his superior. His view that after some twenty years as a priest he could not longer accept the divinity of Christ. His opinion that he could not discover the slightest shred of evidence that Christ had even existed as a historical figure, still less as the greater central figure of the passion, death and resurrection. He found the idea of the crucifixion a remote possibility, though crucifixion was a common form of execution by the Romans, it was not for unorthodox preachers or self-acclaimed prophets. The real point of issue was the doctrine of the resurrection, and hence the salvation of man. The Bishop gazed at him with lively intelligent eyes which reflected little of what he might be thinking, but then neither did they register hostility or ill-will as he might have expected. Finally he had completed his statement, a mere formality as the matter had been dealt with in a frequent exchange of letters over the last year. His presence and the speech he was compelled to make, were simply to guage to what degree, if any, his difficulties were of an abberational nature or, more likely, emotional in origin.

The Bishop offered him some water, saying tea would soon arrive. He declined politely. Silence settled between them, the Bishop's eyes fixed steadily on a worn patch of carpet as if emeshed with all its threads lay the answers to their problems. Logs collapsed in a shower of sparks, many of which shot like minute meteorites and were spent before they reached the pile of the heavy scorched carpet immediately before the fire. He noted that no clock disturbed the quiet of the room. Only the chimes of the city's noted protestant cathedral had penetrated their conversation so far and now for some time at least they too had been silent. On a large round table further down the room to the left of the Bishop, stood a magnificent bunch of chrysanthemums in a large cut glass vase. They splayed out in a splendid show of bronze. Even at that considerable distance they caught and reflected the firelight and when the flames were at their brightest the flowers seemed ablaze. Rain continued to spatter the window panes; sharp, short, above all, insistent.

The Bishop made a slight despairing gesture. His large episcopal ring glittered brilliantly in the rapidly darkening room as night, indisputable and final, fell outside and accurately reflected the inner state of his visitor.

"Tell me, Father, what would you do if you were relieved of your duties? Where would you go? What would you do? How

would you live?" The questions sharp and pertinent, the voice of
the man asking them, cold, emotionless.

The priest stared at the window. In irregular applications of
grey the rain was still streaking down its panes. His own voice,
soft, tiny, not quite timorous. "I have a small amount of money,
my lord. A bequest from my mother. I could live on it for some
time at least. I would not be destitute."

"And then?" The old man stretched forward in a gesture of
assurance or sympathy and laid his hand on the other's knees.
The priest shruddered. His revulsion was immediately obvious to
the Bishop who withdrew his hand but not before he had felt the
steel-strength in the bones of the rather stubby hand of his
superior. "And then, Father?"

The priest now gestured despair with a slight toss of the hand
like a conjurer apparently extracting from nowhere a white dove
and launching it into flight before an astonished audience. He
could not meet the eyes of the man who sat almost directly
opposite him, whose stare in the darkness had the sharp glitter of
a cat's and were not without cunning. He defensively shifted his
gaze to a portrait of one of the Bishop's predecessors that hung on
the far wall. It was tolerably visible in the reflected light. The fire
had lost much of its impetus and the sounds of the city outside
were softened by the ceaseless rain. There was a polite rap on the
door which evoked no response.

The Bishop seemed oblivious of the knock. It was repeated,
less softly than before. This time the Bishop noticed. He jolted
visibly as if he had been about to fall asleep. "Come in," he called
quietly. The door opened. His secretary, a young man he had met
on arrival at the Palace, entered the room bearing a large silver
tray. "Your tea, my lord," he said, laying it on the table between
them. The secretary was about to pour when the Bishop
intervened. "We will serve ourselves, Father, thank you." The
secretary smiled and withdrew. "Please help yourself, Father,"
the Bishop said, rising and going behind his desk. He took a sheaf
of letters from a paper folder and stood there in the dim light of
the slumbering fire, now a mass of pink, twinkling wood. "Shall I
pour for you, my lord?" The Bishop stared at him, blinking
uncertainly then smiled warmly. "Oh yes. Please. If you wouldn't
mind." He returned to reading the sheaf of letters in the folder.
The visitor poured tea into cups and then realised that he did not
know if the Bishop took milk and sugar. There was a plate of
sliced currant cake and a dish of butter pats nearby. He was
ravenous but felt unable to further disturb the Bishop. "Please
help yourself, Father. Don't stand on ceremony. I will see to

myself in due course." Gratefully he took tea and a slice of
fruitcake which he buttered with the self-consciousness he had
always felt when taking afternoon tea in the sitting room of
'Rathbolgan' with his aunts and uncles. The Bishop slipped on a
pair of glasses and continued to read, his lips forming the words
as though he read aloud. The rest of the room was in darkness.
Stealthily he helped himself to more cake and succeeded in eating
it before the Bishop, sighing, laid aside the papers and returned to
the seat he had previously occupied, slipping his glasses into a
scuffed spectacle case which he laid with churchly solemnity on
the table between them. The priest sat upright. His back was not
now supported by the back of the chair. He lent forward, his
elbows resting heavily on the armrests of the chair. He stared
intently through the window, the panes were now white with
condensation, night densely black beyond. He sipped his tea and
watched the Bishop, he himself having no wish to initiate any
conversation.

The Bishop again sighed, gazed at him for a few seconds and
then pointed towards a standard lamp directly behind and to the
left of where he was seated. "Perhaps you would be kind enough
to switch on the lamp for me, Father." He rose to comply. He
returned to his seat which was well beyond the periphery of light
shed by the lamp. Gratefully he realised that his own face now
would be in shadow and his superior would have difficulty in
seeing his expression. The Bishop, wrapped in silence, played
absently with the pectoral cross at his chest. Even without the
glory of his liturgical dress he was an imposing figure, and the
visitor believed, a compassionate man.

The traffic in the streets outside had decreased steadily. Away
beyond the well landscaped gardens of the palace lay the city
shrouded in darkness, a darkness intensified by the heavy rain
falling from the black clouds impacted above. Here and there
diffuse circlets of light which he took to be the street lighting, were
visible. A haze of light hung above the valley city and above the
suburbs. The Bishop stirred. All weariness and abstraction had
fallen from him as though he had shed a skin. Visible in its stead
was the shrunken frame of an old man of great strength of
purpose and above all, of decision. He addressed the priest
forcefully, almost harshly, as though delivering a judgement.

"I have examined your case, Father. I have considered it most
carefully indeed. My conclusion after both prayer and reflection
is that there seems to be no distinct loss of faith, no real apostasy
as it were. In my long experience of dealing with men in Holy
Orders I have found that those who lose their faith do not feel

obliged to honour their vows of poverty, chastity and obedience. Vows in short, made to a God whom they no longer profess to believe." He shook his head in protest, he tried to speak. The Bishop silenced him with a movement of his hands as though stilling turbulent waters over which he had full command. "It is my belief that you are in a dark period of your spiritual life. A testing time as it were, from which I know your faith will emerge strengthened and enriched a thousand fold." The priest uttered a low cry of distress. The Bishop, undeterred, continued. "I am denying your request that you be relieved of you duties. I am in fact imposing upon you in holy obience all the responsibilities of your position as a parish priest, the shepherd of your flock. I place their spiritual welfare in God's hands and in yours, Father, in the knowledge that you will attend to these dutifully and devotedly, and that you will at all times and under all circumstances strive to meet these demands as fully and humanely as possible."

The Bishop paused. After some moments he continued. "I am conscious of imposing a terrible burden on your shoulders . . . an affliction . . . a cruelty perhaps, but I am convinced God will not fail you, nor you He. I believe that from your spiritual darkness and the solemn discharge of your duties great graces will accrue, not only to you but to all in your care." He paused for some minutes now, during which neither of them spoke. When he again spoke his voice was infinitely sad. "May God have mercy on you Father James Fitzgerald. You are about to suffer crucifixion, but I believe you will suffer also the joy of resurrection. If not in this life, then in the next. May God bless and strengthen you for what lies ahead."

The priest gazed at the man denying his right to his own life and demanding a life of servitude instead. He bowed his head and the tears were like brine on his lips. A high wind was blowing now and driving the rain before it. It assaulted the window panes in sporadic onslaughts.

"Perhaps you would care to stay the night, Father? The weather is most inclement. A more substantial meal and a warm bed would not go amiss?"

"I have a train to catch, my lord. It would be most unfair to my priests if I were to stay away for the night. I think it wisest to return."

"Of course. I see. Perhaps I could call you a taxi?"

"I'd prefer to walk, my lord."

"As you wish, Father. As you wish."

The Bishop got to his feet, ending the audience.

Numb and indecisive, the visitor rose. The Bishop extended his hand with the episcopal ring gleaming on it. As always with Romans, he exacts a full tribute, he thought bitterly as he knelt and kissed the ring. He thanked his Bishop formally and haltingly, aware of the dull clod of despair buried deeply in his bowels. The Bishop shook hands. "Pray for me daily, Canon, daily. And take care of your health. You eat well, I take it?"

"Moderately well, my lord."

"Good digestion, the key to good health. And buttermilk. Drink at least a pint a day if at all possible. Most nutritious."

They parted wordlessly at the parlour door. Behind him it was silently but firmly closed. He was helped into his coat by the Bishop's secretary, a smiling young man of such robust good health and vibrancy, he found it difficult to guess how young he was. The visitor blinked in the harsh light of an old Waterford chandelier adapted to electricity. A brash effect. The secretary informed him it was a bad night outside. He agreed that yes, indeed, it was. The youth suggested that he call a taxi from the rank down on the bridge. He declined, politely and firmly, and was handed his furled umbrella with the suggestion that it would be unwise to open it. The wind would undoubtedly destroy it. He agreed but said that he might be able to cope with his hat. The youth beamed in relief. Bidding each other good night — which they had just agreed it was not — they parted, the secretary shutting the front door behind him as he slipped into the night.

He started back, virtually swept off his feet by the force of the wind and the stinging rain. He was aware, but only dimly and remotely, that he was weeping freely, as though it was a matter of no importance, as if he was in fact viewing from a great distance another man for whom he felt no great affinity or affection. He passed through the gates of the ungainly heap which it pleased the faithful of the city, most of whom lived in wretched filth, to call "The Palace". Outside the full fury of the gale struck him. Wave after wave of stinging rain struck him with considerable force but he stood his ground. Taking off his glasses he gazed at the city nestling in the valley below. It huddled on either side of the broad river which branched into several tributaries before coming together again further downstream, to form a swift flowing body of deep water which swept silently to the mouth of the harbour and the choppy waters of the Atlantic beyond. Without spectacles the electric lights atop the poles appeared as large, circular blobs of light, their peripheries blurred and indistinct. It was the city of his birth and the scene of his childhood. He loved it deeply and affectionately as he had loved few human beings with the notable exception of his mother and John. He saw beneath the ugly squalor its opulent beauty in the early eighteen-eighties when it was prosperous and the proud capital of the southern province. He was acutely lonely and he felt a need which was achingly painful to meet once more his parents and John, but they were all dead he told himself bitterly, buried in the bleak stretches of St. Joseph's Cemetery across the river. He recalled his mother's deep love at least in the early years of his life, which he so amply reciprocated, she shared his vision of becoming a priest. She lived to see the day and he had given her his blessing as with his father she knelt on the pebbled drive before the diocesan seminary, a faded remnant of the once vibrant person she had been. His father, correct, cold, showing no emotion whatever, dabbing at his pale blue eyes which watered excessively. His voice, formal, removed. "Splendid, my boy. Splendid" as though he had run a hard race well.

She was of planter stock and her family had been active in the affairs of the city and the province on the loyalist side for many centuries. They counted some three Lord Mayors amongst their ancestors and a baggage train of relatives who had served in the British Army in many countries of the far-flung empire. They also sported some protestant clerics — one in particular who had risen to become Bishop of Delhi — and the most legendary figure in the family, a major who had fought beside Wellington on the field at Waterloo and whose written description of the battle and its aftermath was still extant when he was a child. He had read it and though he could never grasp the intricate manoeuvres he did remember the passages which described the surgeon-dentists who infested the corpse-strewn battlefield and with savage greed pulled the healthy teeth from all the bodies they could find, to be shipped back to London in crates for resale as teeth of the finest enamel. In the hope of frightening him John read aloud the letter one dark evening in the library at 'Rathbolgan'. He was not at all scared, merely hideously fascinated by the information.

His mother's marriage to his father, who was a Catholic, had caused great bitterness between both families at the time. It had taken place before the promulgation of the papal decree *Ne Temere* which dictated that all the children of a religiously mixed marriage be brought up as catholics. Until then the boys of a family were brought up in the faith of their father and the daughters in that of their mother, which whilst it satisfied no one, was in many ways more civilised. She lived to see the decree made but its implications were well beyond the limits of her intellect then. His father had been the son of a small builder who specialised in church building; by broadening the basis of his father's business he had risen rapidly until he was on equal footing with the older, better established and for the most part, protestant businessmen; he demanded and received in the teeth of ferocious opposition many of the municipal buildings contracts. He was elected to the city council as a nationalist though not as a Home Ruler.

Their marriage had been a happy one and only the death of John, the elder son, had marred it, or perhaps more correctly destroyed what happiness they had hitherto enjoyed. John was a medical student of considerable brilliance at the city's University and a superb athlete who had set a number of College records including a national record in the half mile. Much was expected of him by both his parents and all who knew him at the University. An expert swimmer, he drowned in the broad stretches of the Blackwater near his mother's home at 'Rathbolgan'. It was a clear summer's evening and the stretch of river where his body was recovered was quite untreacherous. His death was and remained inexplicable. He lay in St. Joseph's cemetery out there in the Stygian darkness and teeming rain which now completely obscured the priest's view.

His mother's town house, 'Templeton', stood on the same heights on which he now stood. It was quite the most favoured neighbourhood in the city, set as it was on the hillside and commanding a view of the city below and the river as it left the confines of the quays and swept towards the harbour some miles downstream. He still had some elderly cousins living there and elsewhere in the city, but since the nationalist issue had driven a wedge between partisans of both persuasions they had long ceased to meet though he was not extremely nationalistic.

He cherished only one thing in particular about his childhood and his protestant relatives, the memory of those days he had spent at their home at Rathbolgan, the beautiful Georgian mansion in which his mother had been born and which stood in woodlands on the banks of the Blackwater some miles outside that most English looking of Irish towns, Fermoy.

Considered a splendid example of its kind, it was now a ruin open to wind and weather, burned by the more extreme republicans during the Civil War. He had spent the happiest days of his life working through the summer on the estate, or so he had fondly thought. He had in fact been merely tolerated by his older cousins and the workmen who had indulged him. John, on the other hand had been accepted by all at their level; an expert horseman, he was capable of managing animals of all kinds and more than earned his keep during the harvest time with his zest and ability for exhausting labour; he won the admiration of even his grandfather, who freely admitted to his prejudiced belief that the distinguishing characteristics of papists were a whelp-like devotion to a bigoted priesthood, a dislike of hard work and necks which on inspection proved to be invariably dirty. John they had loved and admired, he so much younger had been merely tolerated.

He dismissed the memories of the past which crowded in about him. They were always an unsettling influence and since his very early days as a priest he had disciplined himself to avoid friendships of too strong and binding a nature — and he admitted to himself, too wounding a nature also — that he might become a more perfect instrument of the Christ. Now he yearned to renew his ties with the past, if only fleetingly. He thought of daring to visit 'Templeton' but since only the very aged could expect to remember him, he would not risk the embarrassment of presenting himself to total strangers and possibly risking a resounding rebuff.

He turned towards the town, hungry but loath to enter a hotel and take a meal amongst drenched, chattering people who frequented hotels on such nights and who chatter like excited geese while consuming expensive meals. He headed into the wind and walked slowly downhill, head bent against the stinging rain, towards the centre of city which for him had lost all the charm and elegance it had possessed in his childhood and now seemed squalid and dirty and overrun by poverty-stricken people. It, he reminded himself, had suffered badly, as his father had always stoutly maintained it would, by the withdrawal of the British garrison, their departure depriving the local farmers and the city merchants of a profitable source of revenue. It had suffered also gross physical damage in the sack of the city centre during the War of Independence. It had paid dearly, as his father maintained it would, for its republican sympathies.

He gained the lower level of the valley and crossed the bridge. To the east lay ships anchored at the quays. He remembered how as a child he watched for hours on end the ceaseless activity of the river and thought himself handsomely rewarded for all his patience if a ship docked or cast-off. He had longed to be on one of them and had dreams of long voyages to remote and romantic places he knew only as names on his Great Atlas Of The World. That book had been a gift from his mother after he had ceased to believe in Santa Claus and was allowed to express a certain preference when it came to Christmas gifts; superbly bound in deep blue leather, it had beautiful etched and coloured plates, and had been one of the real delights of his childhood. He chose a ship while down on the quays and having decided upon a destination he would trace its voyage across the Atlantic or through the Panama Canal out into the massive spread of the Pacific Ocean which he mistakenly imagined to be a vast body of blue, tranquil waters.

The scene struck him as sordid now. Something squalid and mean repelled him since the day when wandering towards the quays, hoping to see a ship slip its moorings and ease into the deeper waters of the river and effortlessly downstream until lost from sight, he had met a young man who bore a superficial resemblance to John. He had introduced himself in uncertain English as a sailor of a German vessel *The City of Hamburg.* His hair was fair, almost bleached white from the sun. He had a deep tan and lively blue eyes which had a coldness about them. The stranger smiled, he remembered, but not with his eyes. He questioned the young boy carefully about his family background, where he lived, how far from home he was and which direction his home lay. He had soon discovered the boy's love of the sea and all things maritime and had offered to take him aboard ship to show him, in particular, the engines which as chief engineer were his special care.

He had readily agreed and when his companion had taken him by the hand, had held it tightly in his, he had found it strange but not unpleasant. It was a pleasure to be in close physical contact with someone as admirable as his companion. The sailor exercised considerable charm as he spoke of his voyages to the most exciting destinations at the ends of the earth, of the adventure of sea life, and the pleasure in having in his care the magnificent engines which drove the ship. Not until they veered away from the quays and he found himself passing through a strange neighbourhood did he begin to suspect that something was amiss. The houses were dilapidated and stank of bodily sweat, boiling potatoes and sour cabbage water. He tried to ease his hand from that of the man but the man's hand was tightly clasped about his, his jaw was set and he was walking rapidly. He protested that they were going in the wrong direction but his companion assured him that they were taking a short cut which would bring them out further down river close to where his ship lay.

Then they chanced upon some waste ground. The man dragged him amongst high, vigorous weeds and a mass of wild grass and in behind a ramshackle hut almost completely covered in a wild briar in full flower. He still remembered the silence of the place, the low hum of bees gathering pollen, the warmth of the wall against which he was pinioned. The man squatted and, lapsing into German, began to whisper softly to him and to caress him gently. Intimately from time to time the sailor kissed him fully and longingly on the lips. He had thought it all so strange but pleasing, very pleasing until the man had bared himself and rapidly exciting himself had climaxed, taking infinite care to soil neither of their clothes. The man had held him then and wept bitterly and hurt him by the tightness of his embrace. The sailor broke from him, adjusted his clothing and walked away very quickly. Stunned, he remained where he was for an indefinite period. Then he became aware of an old man leaning on the window-cill of one of the delapidated houses who was watching him while slowly drawing on his stubby, clay pipe, his face cleft in a broad, malicious grin. He realised with a flood of shame that the old man had witnessed the entire episode. He stumbled across the waste ground trying to escape, to find his bearings.

Eventually he had asked a fat, unpleasant woman who slowly walked towards him down the sunlit side of the street. She smelled of dirt and sweat and when he asked her for directions, she asked where he lived. When he had told her, she deliberately spat into the nearby gutter and barefoot padded on, incurious to misfortune. Later a respectably dressed man stopped and questioned him. Breaking into tears he explained his plight but omitted to tell of his experience with the sailor. The man spoke sternly, warning him against the danger of rambling about such a neighbourhood, then he brought him back to the main street and a more familiar area where he insisted on putting the boy on a tram which would take him part of the way home.

He thought a great deal about the incident. He had been very lonely since John's death. The sailor's charm and something about him physically appealed greatly to him. He had not found his caresses and kisses in any way repellent or unpleasant ....
What had frightened him had been the man's sexual excitement and climax.

He had previously experienced close contact only with his mother who, when he had been younger, frequently kissed him directly on the lips lingeringly before turning out the lamp in his room; leaving him to fall asleep delighting in the sweetness of her lips, the freshness of her breath, and the fragrance of her body which smelled faintly of perspiration and the delicate violet perfume she wore more often than any other. Then one night she kissed him shortly on the cheek, refusing to kiss him on the lips as before. He asked why and stroking his hair she had told him it was wrong of 'young men' to kiss their mothers on the lips. She had spoken as if he would fail to understand but somehow he had, and had sensed acutely the sadness with which she had spoken. It had pierced him, that sad refusal and he had wept when she had left him. He felt himself dispossessed and deceived in a manner he found difficult to efface or excuse. In later years he realised that German had spoken to him as would a man to his lover and he became aware in himself of a sense of despoilment which he had never quite succeeded in exorcising.

He shuddered now on recalling the encounter and told himself that if he met that sailor today they might have something in common, a sense of inner exile and enforced alienation from the world which they inhabited and from those with whom circumstances forced them to live. He thought he might find acceptance with that stricken young man, understanding rather than debased and perverting pity, or even compassion which in the end inevitably proved impotent in the face of what evoked it most. He reflected briefly on how much he needed acceptance and decided his need was so great he dare not dwell on it for any length of time or it would destroy him. He was unlikely ever to receive it, he who had so often rebuffed the simple people who were prepared to extend to him as priest their generosity of heart and spirit in return for courtesy, good-will or even civility. These he had withheld all his life because he had thought it unfitting that he should cultivate friendship in the belief that his soul should be exclusively the abode of the Divine.

He had at first in the early days of his ministry experienced the growth of love, an inner peace and tranquility and a deep compassion which belied his nature by its mere existence and its startling intensity. For a while he believed he had walked with God and excluded all human affection for the sake of the one love which they were taught as seminarians would never fail or falter. But it had both faltered and failed. Now it was dead dust and on his tongue he tasted the bitterness of black ash, the residue of dead loves and lost beliefs. In his heart he believed he could never know a resurrection of any kind, no renewal from any source. He thought of seeking a church in one of the seedier parts of the city to find out if perhaps the simple faith of the worshippers, however few they might be, would strengthen him for the dark nights ahead and the bleak years which would henceforth be his lot. It would be futile he realised. An exercise he could carry out any Saturday evening at his own church when all who had sinned sought absolution, all who suffered sought relief and all who were grieved sought consolation and an end to their unappeasable pain.

Instead he made his way to one of the cinemas in the city centre and without looking at the display board bought himself a ticket to one of the seats in the expensive section in the hope that not only would they be more comfortable but less crowded; there he would not be encompassed on all sides by a stink of sweating couples mingled with the sickeningly sweet, cheap perfumes of the women. The film was a detective story but it failed from the start to catch his attention; he had been correct in assuming that the dearer seats would be less crowded and he found for the first time during that entire day that he was relaxing. Tension was ebbing away like a sly, sullen tide from a high beach. His mind was empty of all thoughts. Images of the past and of the eventful day now ended flitted across his mind. They passed without rational sequence or any effort on his part to muster them into a cohesion which might be of some talismanic significance to him. He discovered to his astonishment contentment and felt as though he would have no longer to seek or find what lay beyond all mortal reach.

Later he ate a hearty meal at a small hotel that was prepared to feed him at so late an hour. Having missed both the last train and bus back to the town, he summoned a hackney motor and was driven home the twenty or so miles through the vale of the river which gave its name to the area and to the town. It was relatively expensive but he was indifferent to what others might consider inexcusable self-indulgence. He slept deeply and in the morning approached the altar to commence his mass in the understanding that he did not believe but duty demanded he faithfully observe all the rituals and unflinchingly shoulder all the responsibilities of his position. Deserts, he reminded himself, bloomed briefly but beautifully after the slightest shower of rain. He thought it worthwhile to live what remained of his fruitless life in the hope, however remote, that he might experience such a blossoming. He, a disbeliever, might yet know the divine in man and briefly, a state of grace.

Having positioned the chalice on the altar he retraced his steps and genuflecting, he blessed himself and announced aloud in Latin that he would enter the altar of God. The God who gaveth joy to his youth.

4

Sunlight streamed through the window of his room. Outside in the first flush of summer the garden was gaily colourful and everywhere the fresh greenery of trees was strikingly clear. By his feet, in the trapezoidal wedge of sunlight on the dark linoleum and the bare varnished boards about it, Bran lay contentedly dozing. One of his eyes was closed, the other open. An ear was erect listening for the slightest sound or disturbance. The heat absorbed by the setter's well brushed coat smelled pleasantly as did the black cloth of the cassock the Canon wore while he sat in an armchair and basked in the strong sunlight. Normally the priest disliked direct sunshine and invariably sought the shade, but today he needed the sunshine, though why he could not say.

The smell reminded him of Saturday night ironing which had been an unvarying ritual in 'Marino'. He had a momentary vision of the flagstoned kitchen with its huge, sparkling range which was kept burning all through the year. He saw Hannah, a big, fresh country girl from outside Charleville, sweating freely as each week she strove to iron the pile of clothes despite the fact that most linens and anything of good quality was sent to the laundry every week. The iron was one of the old fashioned ones with a hollow body into which was slipped a white hot brick from the range fire. She always kept to hand a bowl of water with which she liberally sprinkled the article and then ironed over the dampened patch. The hiss and the smell of steam as she did so was one of the first of his childhood memories which registered early and permanently. Another was of waking up warmly tucked into his bed and hearing the sounds of Hannah raking the range and filling it first thing in the morning as she began, he realised only in retrospect, what was a long arduous day in the kitchen, only one in a life of harsh drudgery.

As a treat he was allowed by Hannah to enter the kitchen which was usually forbidden him. She was a kind, expansive young woman, healthy and cheerful, she was grateful for the opportunity to work for a good employer. She served as maid and cook and had the help of two 'dailies' whom she bossed about a good deal. In return for her labour she was given a small annual payment, good food, and had all to herself a rather bleak room in the attic which was without a fireplace. She also received sensible clothing calculated to last her for at least five years and therefore never very fashionable. She was expected to consult his mother about all her personal clothing even if she did buy it out of her own money. She could not be permitted to dress flashily and so attract what his mother called 'Johnnies' in no uncertain contempt. She received also some of his mother's cast-offs which she sent to her family and which she herself was forbidden to wear. She frequently visited her ailing mother and unmarried sister and was permitted to bake for them a fruitcake or tarts in the summer. She was allowed to take home part of a flitch of bacon which hung from the rafters of the kitchen. The bacon was sent to them by his mother's people from 'Rathbolgan', who also inundated them with a steady supply of country butter, vegetables and summer fruits of all kinds.

Strange, he thought, Hannah like most of the adults of his childhood world are all dead now. He hadn't thought of them in years other than to group them together with all those vague, shadowy figures who had died and for whom in the past he used annually to offer a special mass that they might rest in Christ. For those who might still be living he prayed that they might enjoy good health and suffer no afflictions of the body or mind and that when their end came they might die peacefully and in a state of grace. He saw some of them mentally, just briefly, and what struck him most — given the human capacity for unkindness and indeed outright evil — was their intrinsic goodness, their tenderness to him though he had thought of them then and until now as being dull and commonplace.

Birdsong was audible in the evening air and he told himself that perhaps Catherine also was conscious of birdsong and of the sunlight which so pleased. Recalling the skylight, he hoped they had arranged a shade of sorts otherwise she would be extremely uncomfortable. So strong a flood of light might aggravate her suffering. He remembered her father had had the sense to whitewash the glass to reduce the strength of the glare somewhat. How successful a measure it was he could not imagine. The river waters at the end of the lane he knew from his last visit were low and ran ripplingly over the shallows above the dark pool where the farmers watered their horses in days of prolonged heat. Those, he hoped, would give her some pleasure. They might sooth her mind and help her sleep peacefully and hopefully, they might make her dream happily. But what, he asked himself, would so young a woman have to dream about except perhaps that her approaching death be confounded, her life prolonged and her health sufficiently restored to enable her to just exist, if not live a little longer.

Her disease was growing noticeably acute. He had no idea of her exact state of consciousness. As yet she was not experiencing the great pain which was characteristic of her illness, but already her eyes were sunken and her cheeks hollow and that youthful perfection, which had so struck him when he first saw her, was in some respects fading fast. She was being deeply harrowed. Of that he had no doubt. Yet her face retained a loveliness of sorts. A beauty primarily of the eyes and lips and which was that extraordinary refinement of the dying one sometimes encountered, and for which there could be no physical or supernatural explanation, though people did tend to see in it a sign of holiness and since it proved so great a solace to the bereaved, the belief was never contested.

He visited her three times weekly now and much to his astonishment he look forward to the visits. He relished the moments when, having genuflected before the tabernacle, he took from it the consecrated host and carefully deposited it in the gilted interior of the pyx. The walk to her house was now a pleasure. He experienced something approaching transcendant joy as he approached Copley's Lane, knowing that she was there in her home, hungering intensely for the thin wafer. A longing which at times he found appalling. Did it, he wondered, represent to her food for her shrinking body or, as intended, food for the soul? Was it a last attempt to stave off her death or did she in fact increase in grace? Certainly her devotions after receiving communion were touching and unmistakably sincere. But then was her religion like so many Irish people's, a totally false Christianity erected on the ruins of the pagan temples in which their ancestors had worshipped for far more centuries than they had honoured the Trinity? She found it difficult to pray. Her frame was diminishing and both the brain and its functions were undergoing subtle changes. The response of the body was as yet unknown. What was understood was that the psyche, in all the complex interpretations of that word, did undergo a profound change. Internally, at a level perhaps unrealised by rational man, the mind, the implicit organism that was each living individual, wrestled and sooner or later had to come to terms with infinity and eternity, to prepare for death and extinction. He knew from many conversations with doctors that the body died only when it was ready to do so. Quick death, like that from a bullet or a knife might hasten the complex process but in cases of lingering death the action was visible to those who cared to watch and record it. It was at this very deep level, this almost primordial depth he hoped to reach her and to help her if humanly possible, with the aid of graces which he thought were principally profound insights. So he ministered to her in the hope of gaining some understanding of the divine in man, the penetralia for which all yearned in a bellicose world. To do so he would use the only language of prayer available to him, that of his Church's beliefs and rituals.

It had become his habit to kneel by her bed and whisper to her in a low firm voice the post-communion prayers. She in turn tried with the greatest difficulty to formulate each word, each sentence. It caused her pain to even attempt to speak or in any way communicate. After the prescribed prayers she lapsed into what struck him as a reverie, a state of semi-consciousness, yet her thin fingers rubbed the beads of her rosary. He believed her to be absorbed in an internal meditation equal if not superior to that of verbal prayer. He found himself kneeling far longer than duty or devotion demanded.

The cup of weak tea and biscuits became an established ritual. The mother refused to join him but the fact that he remained in the kitchen with her a little longer each time impressed her, as did having the tea. It comforted her to have him there and so he stayed though he would like far more to retreat to some quite place and then reflect upon the time spent with the dying young daughter.

Sometimes her husband joined them. A big, heavy man, he had been in the Royal Irish Constabulary for the greater part of his adult life. He had been diligent but never excessive. He was never violent or vengeful as were so many of his comrades, he had been known to drag a drunkard home and throw him on his bed and leave him to the care of his wife and family rather than prosecute him for disorderly conduct and abusive language. This had been remembered to his advantage during the political troubles of some twenty years ago and though many of his comrades were shot or burned out of their homes or barracks, he had gone unmolested until one, unsuccessful attempt had been made on his life. He knew quite well that the shooting had been deliberately botched and that the man who had injured him, not seriously, could have killed him. He had married late in life and his wife was in her forties when they married. She bore a child and to protect the child's and his wife's position in the community he resigned his job with loss of all pension rights.

He now made a precarious living working as a part-time gardener for some elderly protestant widows who could no longer afford to employ a man full-time and were unable to do the work themselves. His own garden adjoining the house was larger than the others in the Lane and bigger than one might suspect on first seeing it. It ran right down to the river bank and was well planted with potatoes and other vegetables. The small area in front of the cottage was devoted to flowers of the kinds common to small plots. He was justly valued for the work he undertook and though it afforded him only a pittance he lived on what he earned, sometimes undertaking house repairs and the like, rather than petition the government formed by men who had killed or maimed so many of his colleagues. He was proud and independent and was much respected.

He was a taciturn man; having respectfully sought permission to smoke in his own house, he would fill and pack his pipe with care and lighting it, would settle down to smoke in silence. He affected calmness and strict self-control but his eyes were ravished. He was plainly in despair. He had no means of expressing himself and therefore remained silent. The woman sometimes tried to engage in desultory conversation and made futile attempts at levity. He found her efforts difficult to deal with. He struggled for in a similar tone but his efforts were feeble and sooner or later a cumbrous silence descended on the house, broken only by the kitchen clock on the dresser and very distinctly, the slush of the river made shallower by the spell of continuous good weather, running over the exposed stones, at the end of the Lane. He knew he would never forget that combination of sounds: a ticking clock, the trickling river waters and the deep sighing, quite unconscious, of the mother and father locked in their despair which was at odds with their bland attempts at resignation. The woman — "God is good and so is his Holy Mother", the man — "God's Holy Will be done". And the Canon nodding his head, sharing neither their faith nor hope nor belief in the divine providence.

He found their faith distasteful. The evidence of their eyes alone should have made it clear that the girl was destined to die. He himself had no exceptional reverence for the consecrated host he carried to the dying girl who received it with gladness and devotion. Yet he believed that she was strengthened and comforted by his visits and by her prayers after communion. That itself imbued it with a significance it otherwise would not have. He could not deprive her of its consolation, nor could he deny the parents the solace her reception of it gave them. Paradoxically, he was witnessing in her slow agonising death the growth of what he would have described without hesitation as the grace of God. Now he no longer believed in God, at least not as defined by any orthodox religion, yet it was unmistakable that the girl increased in grace. And it was radiant. Bright and rare and lovely, wonderful to behold and during his time of prayer with her, share in to some extent. He longed to be immersed in it more fully, totally if at all possible. It lifted him spiritually, in a way he thought of as bringing a new meaning of that much abused word. It eased his spirit, his very physical state and in a sense it fructified the inner aridity of his being commonly referred to as the soul. He believed himself privileged to witness such a growth, as though it was a flower, delicately shy and rarely seen by any living person.

The time spent away from Catherine was slowly becoming intolerable to the Canon. Odd, he thought of it — so deep was his sense of deprivation — as a form of crucifixion. He found his mood almost past bearing, haunted as he was by the emptiness of his life after her death. He feared that his will to live might perish with her. She had become the focal point of his entire life, his one preoccupation which overshadowed all others. She was his sustenance.

He started forward, realising that he had fallen asleep. Bran glanced at him quizzically. The light of day was fading from the scene before him. Guard Mullins was watering his vegetables. His shirt was the vivid green of the regulation issue to all Civic Guards. His sleeves were rolled up, his pipe clenched between his teeth. The drizzle from the hose was audible as it seeped into the parched earth and fell upon the shallots. It was proving to be a fine summer and promised an abundant harvest. That much was something to be grateful for in a world at war and one in which it was impossible to forget the havoc being wreaked upon innocent civilians on both sides engaged in the conflict.

He suddenly remembered the encounter with the impertinent young fellow whom he had struck the first day he called to the girl's home. The boy's parents had made a formal complaint to the Guards. Both parents were illiterate and he hadn't the slightest doubt that Whelan the republican had been responsible for the charges being pressed officially. Neither parent of their own accord would have dared to act against their parish priest. He felt revulsion for Whelan surge inside him. Whelan, he felt, illustrated his father's theory that in times of civil unrest, like a stock-pot being boiled, scum rose to the surface. Undesirables were likely to gain power and authority for which they were unfitted and if anything worthwhile was to be accomplsihed, the scum had to be ladled off and quietly disposed of, the undesirables had to be weeded out and deprived of their position of power. Mr William T. Cosgrave, he reminded himself with satisfaction, had done just that in the suppression of the more radical republicans and had restored law and order and advanced the Church to its proper honoured position in the affairs of the new State. The majority of the people had supported Cosgrave in his admirable efforts. A small minority, corrupted by the alien tenets of socialism then infecting Europe like a deadly pestiferous scourge, trailing famine and civil unrest, did not. Ireland had been spared communism, he thought, due to the resolute action of a few men of faith.

He rose and took off his soutane and his clerical stock and collar, anxious to shave. He glanced at the mantlepiece. Mrs O'Sullivan should appear at any moment with his mug of shaving water. He waited impatiently, blinking in what he now found to be the uncomfortable, harsh, sunlight. He partially drew down the blinds and sat on the bed, his irascibility and aggravation growing each passing moment. He whistled softly and absently as he sometimes did. It was, he thought idly, a trait he had inherited from his father. He had a fleeting glimpse of that cold, unaffectionate man who seemed incapable of loving anyone, other than John perhaps. Somewhat to his surprise he could hardly recall his father's image in anything other than blurred outline. Other than his massive head of silver-white hair, his rather cold pale blue, almost grey, eyes, the other details remained indistinct and he could not recollect them.

He glanced at the clock again and found that it was past the quarter hour. She should be here by now, he told himself and as so often happened nowadays, he found his gorge rising to an unwarranted pitch. These rages which were becoming more frequent, frightened him by their intensity. They threatened to overwhelm him and on at least two occasions he had lost consciousness very briefly. He would have to consult Doctor Barrett about them when they dined later in the evening. If he were to lose consciousness during the mass it would give rise to public scandal and would have to be reported to the Bishop. He had no great desire for contact with the Bishop, or his secretary for that matter. Since he had last visited the Palace both parties had decided to let matters rest as they were. A rather blunt summary of his relations with his Bishop, but apt nevertheless.

His health had evidently deteriorated in the last year. He slept badly and when sleep did come it was fitful and he constantly dreamed of the dead and his childhood days. Again and again he found himself dreaming variations of one persistent theme. He was in a pony and trap or possibly a motor car, some means of conveyance which he could never quite determine. He was being driven, in a sense propelled, towards 'Marino', the home of his childhood. It was always day and the entire landscape was bathed in a magical, pale golden luminesence. The scene of his dream bore no resemblance to the typographical details of the real place. The approach to 'Marino' the long avenue of walled gardens surrounding the isolated houses, each sheltering behind screens of trees and spreads of well card-for lawn. Yet unmistakably he was nearing 'Marino' and his mother was alive. He experienced a great joy knowing that once more he would see her. The tall, majestic woman with rich black hair, vivacious eyes, the fine expressive lips and ungainly hands which to some slight degree spoilt her beauty and of which she was over-conscious. People, he knew from experience, soon forgot those hands. Most, he had observed, were riveted by her features, enhanced as they were by her fine dark hair gathered at the back and held in position with a silver clasp in the French manner which owed nothing to the fashion of the day. He found it difficult during his waking hours to analyse the ecstatic delight at the possibility of seeing his mother again in the dream state, her face pacific and serene, her bearing grand and upright, her eyes shining brightly as she smiled gently and extended her hand, and grasping his tightly and warmly before allowing herself to be kissed. Her voice soft, silvertoned, musically modulated as she spoke. "James! How wonderful to see you again. How very well you look."

He never did arrive at 'Marino' in his dreams. He did approach the house along its pebbled drive with stately elms flanking and almost meeting overhead to form in summer a bower of green foliage, a mysteriously cool arcade through which beaten lemon sunlight seeped and lay on the ground in dappled pools. He never entered the hallway to have his coat taken from him by Hannah and laid on the great oaken table. He never entered the drawing room, its high windows open, top and bottom, a faint breeze stirring the lace curtains gently, dreamily, the air pungent with the smell of arum lillies which she loved above all other flowers though in popular mythology they were not the resurrectionary flowers of Easter but the tributary flowers of the pagan dead, and therefore unlucky. He never approached to kiss her or have his hand so warmly taken. Just when expectancy for what lay ahead was most acute, the mood of the dream invariably mutated and he experienced that sharp stab he had first known when fully conscious. Death came stealthily: turning aside with a soft cry of anguish, despair and great pity in her eyes, she died. Kneeling by her bed he imparted absolution, proffered her soul to the Godhead and intoned the prayers conclusory of a Christian life, that she might know above all else eternal rest.

Sometimes when the memory of the dead was aroused he wept in the privacy of his room and in the shelter of darkness, or else he stirred himself, switching on the feeble light above his bed to read a detective novel because he had discovered that if he did not immediately distract himself and dispel the sense of despair which overcame him, he would succumb and spend the day in futile grief. A sorrow made all the more harrowing by the fact that his mother had died spiritually long before her actual death. In the last years of her life following the death of John she had become a wretched shell. Untidy and unkempt, she lapsed into extreme decrepitude. Her hair lost its lustre, her facial beauty faded rapidly, her lips had somehow become thin and rather mean, and most of all, her eyes were dulled, lifeless as if glazed and she was compelled to see life through a murky mist or a dark, distorting prism. Her mind was affected also. She sat for hours on end in her bedroom, a shabby shawl draped about her shoulders, her hands cradled in her lap as though broken at the wrists, her mouth slack, her jaw hanging, dribbling ceaselessly, while she stared ahead into vacant space. In her better moments when some spark of her former vitality asserts itself she spoke of John as though he were alive and was shortly expected. Sometimes he sat with her during such periods and confusing him with John her eyes would brighten, her voice took on that silver tone which he so loved to hear and she would flow fleetingly, happiness and release. He tried to sustain the horrible fiction to afford what relief he could but his voice invariably betrayed him and in turn, feeling herself betrayed, she would moan softly swaying to and fro on the edge of her armchair, keening like one stricken in the manner of the old shawled women in the squalid hovels of the city, when confronted with their dead. How he had hated her despite his efforts not to when she mistook him for John and showed such delight and pleasure, such unqualified love.

There was, he realised, a peculiar force at work. His mind was in some way being affected. He was constantly thinking of the young girl. He always thought of her as a girl rather than as a lady — which was the fashion of his time — wasting away in her bed under the skylight in her room and at the same time the past was exercising a fascination and, more seriously, a power over him such as he had never known before. It was as though a cleavage of the mind took place. He saw and lived anew the past. He recalled in great detail old scenes of his youth and saw in vivid detail those he had known, in some instances loved, who were now dead. He recalled their voices, their gestures, the way they sat at the dinner table or entered or left a room. He found it enticing though he knew it was not without danger. He increasingly believed that somewhere in the convoluted past lay the answer as to how best to deal with his present and so safely chart a course through the troubled waters which he believed lay ahead of him. That knowledge taken in conjunction with his relationship with the young girl he hoped would end his inner sterility, the sense of futility which so dogged him increasingly. He again resolved to bring the matter up discreetly when he dined with Dr Barrett later in the evening.

He glanced at the clock. It was now on the half hour and still his housekeeper had not brought his shaving water. Irritably he drew on his dressing gown and left the room. He passed along the landing and came to the May altar erected by Father Good with his somewhat reluctant permission, as part of his crusade to have the people in the parish erect similar altars to Mary, Queen of Peace, that they might become focal points for daily prayers for peace and the banishment from their midst of atheistic communism. The blue mantled figure of Mary was surrounded by a profusion of flowers in receptacles of all kinds. The children of the town, having heard him preach his crusade at both the convent and national schools, called frequently to Mrs O'Sullivan's dismay, with bunches of flowers which Father Good felt obliged to accept and place at the foot of the statue rather than discard them as common sense might dictate. He scowled at what he thought of as an excess of zeal on the part of the priest. The man was in some respects wanting. His character and masculinity were not sharply defined, they were blurred rather than sketched in bold, black lines as one might expect of a young man of his years. He seemed totally unsuited to the realities of the priesthood and yet, he reflected, he carried the burden of the confessional with an ease that was enviable. He was also a good confessor. Not soft, but one of those blessed with the ability to deal with the human soul at its meanest and dirtiest and somehow remain untouched by the sordidness, the filth, the unutterable pettiness of humanity stripping its hideous wounds and running sores in the sheltered darkness of the box. He himself detested the time he spent couped-up in the confessional. The sin and shame rising from those kneeling behind the grid, he found overwhelming and revolting. As unimaginably disgusting as having to watch someone he knew excrete on the floor tiles of the church. He felt a sense of outrage rise within. Again his heart raced, his head ached unpleasantly, his temple throbbed. He grasped the bannister of the stairs and quickly withdrew his foot from the first thread of the upper flight of steps. He remained still trying to recover his equilibrium. How often had he had to wait alone, confined in that suffocating cubicle which stank of unwashed bodies, foul breath, and sickening guilt-ridden sexuality while Father Good's and Father Phelan's confessionals were virtually besieged. Unwisely he had once given vent to his anger and lacerated those who thought confession a popularity contest and had driven those who had allowed themselves to be coerced, to take their place outside his box. Not all were prepared to be brow-beaten. One or two women had paused at the altar, genuflected and left the church, their heels beating a defiant tattoo as they marched down the aisle. It had been far from an edifying experience and even now he flushed at the humiliation his own intemperate manner had brought upon him. Bracing himself, he made his way downstairs cautiously.

Mrs O'Sullivan was in the kitchen with Father Good. She gaped at him in astonishment as he entered and then reddened with embarrassment. She smelt of sweat in a womanly way and her brow glistened. The range was lit and there was something cooking in the oven. Her coat was slung carelessly over a kitchen chair. Father Good was seated at the table spooning what he termed 'tea-dust' into small paper cones of the kind in which shopkeepers doled out pennyworths of sweets to school children. They exchanged looks of alarm. "Your water, Canon," she exclaimed, "I clean forgot about it." She paused and then added hurriedly, "I was out visiting my sister. You know she had a bad turn a few days ago and she's killed trying to look after the big family. She has ten, Canon, ten altogether." She paused and wiped her hands on her white apron. "I'll bring it to you immediately." He glanced at the plates of salad which she was preparing. A frugal but presentable meal in these days of scarcity and rationing, by no means to be despised. "If you would be so kind, Mrs O'Sullivan. I would appreciate it." His voice was harsh, dictatorial. Not at all as he intended it to be. She bridled at the implied rebuke. Father Good applied himself to his task with all the concentration of a child having just been taught by his elders how to use a bucket to produce perfect sandcastles and now solemnly engaged in the glorious act of creation without supervision. The parish priest thought of tempering his harshness with an enquiry about her sister whom she had just mentioned, but could not pretend to be interested. He abruptly left the kitchen and hurriedly regained his bedroom.

Father Good, he thought, had received a parcel from his family. They owned a number of businesses, amongst them a grocery shop. They unfailingly sent him the scoopings from the tea chests and illegally perhaps, a little of the better quality tea for the use of the parochial household, the dust being distributed amongst the deserving poor, mostly the elderly who found the rationing of tea and tobacco a great deprivation. Father Good flitted about town tapping on the doors of hovels and decrepit cabins with open sewers outside their doors, distributing his little paper cones rather like Christ distributing his loaves and fishes. He was welcome in the homes he visited and spent an hour or so in lively conversation with bedridden old men and women who had lice-infested hair and lay in flea-ridden bedclothes, before departing in a chorus of supplications to another visit. The Canon snorted in contempt: how little the good father knew of the endless capacity of the Irish for spleen and malice, the relish with which they bit the hand that fed them. Passingly he realised he loathed the man for no reason whatever other than that his masculinity appeared diffused. Like an inner growth his capacity for hatred was steadily growing and he was the one being consumed by it.

There was a discreet tap on the door. He called: "Come in," rather coldly. Mrs O'Sullivan entered with a mug of hot water and fresh linen draped over her arm. Her face was flushed but whether she was still smarting over his implied rebuke or from the exertion of climbing the stairs, he could not decide. He thought again of enquiring about her sister but found himself unable to do so. He curtly nodded towards the marble-topped washstand. She laid the mug of water on it and the towel beside it. She was about to leave, then turned to him again and plainly distressed, asked quiveringly, "Will that be all for now, Canon?" "For the moment yes, thank you, Mrs O'Sullivan."

She hesitated uncertainly, then murmuring "Thank you Canon," she left the room. He knew he should make some reference to her sister's state of health. It would lessen her anxiety and perhaps cheer her somewhat. But he was incapable of even so small a grace.

He took off his dressing gown and shirt and laid them aside. He shaved slowly and with great attention. He had a horror of blood and could hardly appear as Father Phelan frequently did, with tiny bits of newspaper stuck all over his lower face where he had nicked himself and thus received a glacial reprimand which despite the man's jollity nevertheless struck home. Having shaved he went to the bathroom and cleaned out the mug; carefully he filled a large basin and brought it back to his room, laid it on the washstand and locked the door. Now began what for him was the most repugnant of daily tasks, his bodywash. He always used cold water but found it difficult to immerse his entire body in a bath. He therefore had to resort to a bowl and hand towel. He took off his woollen vest, now regretting that he hadn't changed to lighter underclothes. It was probably too late to do so. He was likely to catch a bad chill on making such a change. Illness, even in a mild form, he detested. It increased one's dependence on others. He first washed his hands with the same ritual care with which he washed his fingertips before the consecration of the mass. He then cleaned his face and wiped it clear of soap suds. Dipping the flannel cloth in the water, he patted his face all over, his neck and under his arms. He then took off his trousers and underpants and in what was to him the most unpleasant but necessary part of his daily hygiene, he washed his genitals. He was conscious of his own body odours as he dried himself carefully and they nauseated him as strongly as did the odour of others.

He caught a glimpse of his body in the wardrobe mirror. He was thin, possibly underweight, yet his stomach protruded unbecomingly and his white skin struck him as being the underbelly of a garden slug, slimy and unclean. Revolted, he turned away and took fresh underwear from a chest of drawers. He dressed slowly, exhilarating in the cleanliness of the clothes, smelling slightly of carbolic soap. He put on a freshly laundered stock and collar.

The housekeeper appeared on time. She took away the dirty water and returned with a basin of fresh water. When she had left he washed his feet carefully, paying attention to each individual toe. He changed his socks and felt very much better. He decided against summoning her so he emptied and sluiced out the bowl himself in the bathroom. On returning to his bedroom he decided on impulse to dispense with his soutane and slipped on a jacket. He sat in the chair to the left of the empty fireplace, took out his breviary and commenced Matins. He could not concentrate. He saw the printed words with crystal clarity but they failed to register other than as a series of apparently meaningless hieroglyphs. Tired, he laid it aside and lapsed into vacancy. Doctor Barrett's arrival woke him. He was at first confused by his surroundings and was very much aware that he had been dreaming in vivid colour a dream he could not now recall. He heard Mrs O'Sullivan greeting the doctor at the door and in time, their careful footfalls on the staircase. She knocked lightly and

entered on hearing him call 'come in'. "Doctor Barrett to see you,
Canon." She stood aside and his visitor entered the room.
Smiling what he knew from experience was merely a dutiful
smile, she withdrew.

Doctor Barrett approached, his hand outstretched. "Good
evening, Canon. How are you this very pleasant evening?" The
man was dressed in light Irish tweeds, brown boots highly
polished, a wine coloured waistcoat complete with watchchain
and gold fobs, and a rather bright red tie and shirt. A red
bandana, spotted black, hung carelessly from the handkerchief
pocket of his jacket, rather like a gash revealing raw flesh or the
flaming of a tulip against the bleak landscape of early spring.
Even as he advanced in greeting the man's eyes expertly scanned
him from head to heel.

"I'm very glad to see you, Doctor. And very glad indeed you
were able to accept my invitation to dine. I'm afraid I have a
collation rather than a feast for you tonight."

"That will do very well indeed, Canon," he replied pleasantly.
"Very well indeed."

The doctor stood by an armchair, smiling more pleasantly than
professionalism alone would demand. A friendship of a sort
existed between the two men and had for some years, yet they
maintained a formality, a certain distance. There were, it was
understood, certain areas of each others lives which were beyond
trespass. It struck him as odd that though Doctor Barrett smiled
almost expansively, the man's eyes were troubled.

"Please sit down," he said. Since the beginning of the war he
received Doctor Barrett — the only visitor he chose to entertain
with any frequency — in his bedroom rather than in the parlour
or sitting room downstairs, both to conserve fuel and attain as
much privacy as possible without unduly offending the feelings of
others. He had no sooner seated himself than he realised that he
had failed to instruct Mrs O'Sullivan to bring up the drinks tray
and have it ready for his caller as was customary. He attempted to
rise to his feet but found he could not. He sank back into the
chair. His jaw had dropped, his head was shaking violently. He
was unaware that Barrett had jumped to take his pulse. He felt a
slight pressure on the wrist of his right hand and then against the
left temple.

"How long have you been having these spells?" the doctor
enquired sharply. He goggled blankly at the questioner who
stared back at him and then blinked rapidly a few times in
succession, rather like a tabby cat. The doctor seemed to be
making a rapid decision. "Have you been feeling unwell

generally, Canon?"

"Not noticeably," he replied. He realised he was speaking untruthfully but could not retract. Doctor Barrett persisted. "But you have been under some strain recently? More so than usual perhaps?"

He shook his head. He formulated the words. "No. Not that I have been aware of," but when he opened his mouth to speak, he could not do so. His lips quivered. Tears gathered in his eyes and trickled down his face in streamlets. He both saw and felt them. He bowed his head. Sorrow, piercing sorrow racked his entire body. He was aware of Mrs O'Sullivan calling "Dinner is ready, Canon", and of Doctor Barrett opening the door and speaking softly to her. "A little later perhaps, Mrs O'Sullivan. The Canon and I have something urgent to discuss." Her reply, "Of course, Doctor. There's no rush. It's only the bit of salad. It won't spoil ... and I haven't the tea made yet. Whenever you're ready, just let me know." She retreated along the landing. To the Canon everything seemed remote and distant and he seemed in a way a dispassionate observer of his own behaviour.

Doctor Barrett took a slim silver case from the inside pocket of his jacket. "You don't mind if I smoke, Canon?" He shook his head. "A little whiskey perhaps?" He felt it unnecessary to reply. His visitor sat in the chair opposite but he did not turn to face him or even to fleetingly meet his gaze. Doctor Barrett inhaled deeply, then exhaled, opening his mouth wide and watching the smoke bellow forth like smoke from the belly of a dragon; he appeared completely relaxed. "I think you had better tell me about it, Canon. I think you should tell me everything."

The priest spoke haltingly, with difficulty, still choked. "She is mortally stricken, poor, beautiful child. She is cut down in the prime of life ... never having lived. She is not in any great pain but as her illness runs its course she will suffer ... she will suffer greatly before she dies." The questioner quietly, clinically asked: "And this disturbs you?" There was an element of surprise if not astonishment in the doctor's voice. He bowed his head, clutching it between his hands and pushing hard against his forehead. "Yes," he managed to reply. Adding, "My God can you not see?" He moaned. Barrett rose to his feet and called Mrs O'Sullivan. She rushed upstairs, her face showing anxiety. Behind was Father Good, also worried.

"What is it, Doctor?" she asked in a whisper. Barrett held the door behind him half-closed, barring their view of the room and the weeping Canon. He gave her the keys to his car. "You will find my medical bag on the back seat. Bring it to me

immediately." She snatched the keys from him and scurried away
fervently blessing herself as she did so. Father Good glanced
directly at Doctor Barrett. "Is there anything I can do, Doctor?"
He in turn gazed frankly at the younger priest; both were aware
that he and his superior were not on the best of terms. "No thank
you, Father. I think not. Not at this stage." With a nod of his head
he signalled to him to withdraw quietly. Father Good did so
instantly. "If I can be of any help, please call me —" Doctor
Barrett pursed his lips. "I will certainly do that if it is necessary,
Father. Thank you." He returned to the room, took one last
lingering pull on his cigarette and searching for an ashtray, he
stubbed it out, silently watching the man still baying like an
animal and swaying back and forth in the reflex action of extreme
emotional pain. Rarely, he mused, had he seen such a picture of
utter misery and desolation.

All was quiet. Outside all was quiet. Birdsong had ended and
day was slowly fading. He sat down in the chair opposite the
Canon. He thought he had known this priest. Evidentally he did
not. Mrs O'Sullivan called. He opened the door and took his
medical bag from the woman who looked as though she was
about to cry. It was, he thought grimly, not unknown for slaves to
mourn for their masters or bondsmen for their dictators. She
seemed about to make an enquiry but thought better of it and
walked away.

He lay the bag on the bed and unwrapped a hypodermic
needle. He took a metalled topped spirits container from its box.
Opening it he extracted a sterilised needle, one of a number in the
flask-like bottle. He reached for a glass phial and quickly and
expertly snapped off the nipple at the top. He inserted a needle
into it and slowly drew off the contents. He glanced at the Canon.
"I think we had better get you to bed, Canon." The priest
gestured dismissively with his hands. He tried to speak. He failed.
He attempted again. "I have something. Important. To discuss.
With. You." Doctor Barrett nodded. "There will be plenty of
time for that tomorrow. Just now I want you in bed."

He again protested with his hands, but Doctor Barrett was
decisive. "I want you in bed. Right now if you please." The
Canon refused to move. "I must insist, Canon. I have no
alternative."

He helped the still keening man to his feet and holding him
tightly by the forearm, steered him to the bed. He undressed him
as one would a child and like a child the Canon made no protest.
The doctor glanced briefly at the lean, bony body of the man now
naked. His skin was curiously white. Cream-white like that of

rich milk and which a woman might well prize. The visitor slipped a nightgown over his shoulders and flicking aside the covers he eased the old man into the bed between the sheets and pulled the eiderdown up about him. The priest's head sank into the pillow. He heaved a long, deep sigh, a sigh of the very weary, the tired, the sick with life. Doctor Barrett swabbed the bared arm with spirits and said in the measured voice which was his stock in trade: "This will hurt. But only for a little. The more relaxed you are, the less likely it is to cause pain." He punctured the vein with the point of the needle and began slowly to press home the plunger. The Canon's sobbing had ceased. He was silent and looked as though he would have gladly accepted death at that moment. The drug began to take effect. His eyes glazed, his tense body slackened. He spoke with difficulty, his speech seemed to span an ever widening abyss. "Will she suffer greatly?" With a brutal candour he had never thought he possessed, the doctor replied, "Yes, I am afraid she will." The Canon uttered a low cry and lapsed into unconsciousness.

He withdrew the needle carefully and wrapping it, replaced it in his bag together with the empty phial. He lingered on in the darkened room though he knew there was nothing more he could do. He heard the front door open downstairs. The boisterous voice of Father Phelan rang through the house. "Go boy. Go!" Then the voice was cut short. The yapping dog tore up the stairs and began to scratch impatiently at the door. He made no effort to leave him in. The dog barked once or twice, then flopped to the ground and after sniffing vigorously, began to whine in much the same manner as dogs are said to whine on the death of their master. The room was now almost in total darkness though Barrett could still discern the individual pieces of furniture. The figure in the bed was sleeping peacefully, perfectly reposed.

5

He slept dreamlessly, deeply, for what on waking seemed a very long time. His head felt heavy, his mind clouded, and yet he was aware of a state of wellbeing such as he had not experienced since as a boy he had awoken on the nights of torrential rain and high winds which rattled the window panes in his small room; on such occasions he had seen everything bathed in the glow of the night-light which had a ruby tinted glass chimney cover, cut deeply in an intridcate pattern which, as his mother had explained, affected the light shed by the burning candle within as it bathed the room and its furniture. Opening his eyes and seeing the lambent objects of his room he was very grateful that he was safely sheltered and knowing, knowing with that absolute certainty of childhood that his parents were sleeping soundly in their beautiful bedroom on the lower floor and John was asleep in his rather spartan room and Hannah was safely asleep in hers; and he remembered, but could not for a moment imagine, the plight of those dispossessed who he knew, from the subdued conversation of his parents, were sometimes found in archways during the bitter weeks after Christmas, dead from slow starvation and exposure to the harsh and savage elements they could no longer withstand.

He blinked and the brief vision of his childhood bedroom faded and he felt shortly but deeply, loss and sorrow for all which was past. Resonant, assertive sunshine struck the far granite wall of the garden where the trained pear trees heightened the whiteness of the marble which occurred here and there. Mica-shists sparkled in the early morning with all the brilliance and dash of diamonds. Mrs O'Sullivan bustled into the room, good humoured and somehow seeming very tolerant. She spoke crisply and with a confidence which did not belie her appearance.

"Good morning, Canon. You're awake at last. You're looking very well. Nice and refreshed. It's a glorious morning altogether. I'll bring you your breakfast presently." She paused and surveyed him because to her surprise she had addressed him with affection. Then smiling benignly, too much so he thought, she bustled out of the room.

She had scarcely gone when there was a timid knock on the door which identified the caller as Father Good. He found it quite difficult to marshall all his faculties, they seemed scattered but lying within reaching distance like the discarded toys of a bored infant. There was a tendency to drift off into that nether state which, upon reflection, so resembled childhood sleep and the tremendous sense of warmth and security it engendered. There was another rattle at the door but before he could gain sufficient control to speak Father Good entered. He hesitated and glanced about him in trepidation as if the distance between them was a swamp to be negotiated at the peril of his life. He clasped his hands together in what might be described as a sanctimonious manner but which the figure in the bed thought dollish and feminine, though he knew it was done simply to control the trembling hands of the highly strung young priest.

"Good morning, Canon," he said in his soft, shy voice. "I trust you are feeling well." The use of the word trust struck him as stilted for one so young. He felt his old antagonism towards his most junior priest assert itself. With an effort he hid it and replied, "Yes thank you, Father. I had a very good night's sleep."

Father Good goggled at him, mouth open, in surprise for some seconds and then embarrassed or discomforted, he sought to distract him. "The morning light, Canon, it's not too strong for you?"

"No," he replied firmly. "No at all. In fact I rather relish it." He had spoken strongly and it gave him pleasure to realise that he was gaining control of his faculties. The young priest was clearly at a loss for something relevant to say. "Bran is fine, Canon," he murmured rapidly with the desperation of those who are afraid they will say the wrong thing at the wrong time and in the wrong place. "Father Phelan and I took turns in giving him his exercise over the last few days." Horrified, realising he had blundered, he stiffened as though suddenly transfigured to stone.

He was nodding his head in appreciation when the impact of what had been said struck him. He narrowed his eyes and then asked frostily: "Did you say 'days'?"

Father Good swallowed with difficulty. "Yes, I did." His voice was suddenly very weak.

"How many days did I sleep, Father?" he asked testily.

"Three days . . . and four nights in all." His junior looked wretched, as if he had shattered a much loved object of beauty in the drawing-room of someone whose honoured guest he was. He also managed to look as if he infinitely preferred he were elsewhere.

"I was unconscious for three days?" He noted the familiar edge return to his voice.

"Yes, you were." Father Good glanced furtively at the closed door as if contemplating outright flight.

He closed his eyes, obliterating the terrified figure of the priest and his surroundings. He tried to think, to gauge if it was possible to be unconscious for so long and on waking be unaware of the flight of time. He registered only that he had slept deeply and soundly. A good night's rest, he would have thought, but no more. Resentment flared. His mouth suddenly felt dry and unpleasantly coated with a fine scum. "That was very considerate of you both. I much appreciate it. Perhaps, Father, you could pour me a glass of water. My mouth feels dry."

"Of course, Canon," Father Good replied, released. He poured some water from a carafe on the bedside table with all the ebullience of a Moses again striking the rock and bringing forth water, secure in the knowledge that now he would succeed. He offered his superior the glass.

The parish priest tried to move but found himself powerless. He commanded his limbs to obey. They refused. "I'm afraid you will have to help me, Father. I appear unable to move." Suddenly it occurred to him that he might have suffered a cerebal haemorrhage and might be paralysed or otherwise greatly incapacitated. "What happened? What exactly happened?" he demanded.

Father Good blinked uncertainly. "You suffered a nervous breakdown. Doctor Barrett decided it was essential for you to have complete rest. He's been to see you each morning and evening. Each night he gave you something to keep you asleep, an injection I believe. We — that is Father Phelan and I — we kept ..." He lapsed into awkward silence. Emotion flooded him. He could not speak.

"You kept what?" The question was sharp and angry.

"We kept vigil by your bed each night, Father Phelan and I."

"Was my life in danger?" He was fully aware that he was snapping rather than simply asking.

"No, Canon. It was not." Father Good's dejection was complete.

"I see. Thank you. Please ask Father Phelan to be so kind as to call and see me whenever his commitments will permit him. Go now. I feel spent."

"Your water, Canon."

He gestured dismissively. "Thank you. I no longer feel I need it."

Father Good hesitated as though about to speak. The Canon knew that the man's remarks would be of a personal nature and therefore intrusive. He forstalled with an angry glare, asking, "Was there something else?"

Father Good shook his head and acknowledging failure with a feeble smile, departed.

He sank back into the pillows, overwhelmed by physical and mental weariness. He had longed to ask the young priest about the dying girl's health but had considered it prudent not to do so. He tried to think of her christian name which he knew to be ringing and beautiful, evocative in the extreme, but failed. He was confronted by her ravished face, her gaunt features, her stricken eyes and her lips moving slightly in apparent prayer. He realised that he had come to love her dearly in a ways he had never loved anyone before.

His housekeeper entered with a breakfast tray.

"Knock, woman! Knock before you enter a room. It is common politeness and is the custom of this household, and will so remain as long as I am in charge!"

Mrs O'Sullivan glanced at him mildly surprised at his outburst. "But I did knock, Canon. Twice. I thought you had gone back to sleep."

The setter burst in upon them thrashing his tail and barking joyously, his eyes expectant. The dog pawed his protruding elbow. He reached a hand out and stroked the fellow's head. He yelped sharply in increased pleasure. Unaccountably, he thought of the pigeon he had seen die in flight and fall practically at his feet, its warm heart forever stilled. He again succumbed to the pity which had overcome him on that occasion and dripped tears as though the presence of Mrs O'Sullivan was of no great consequence.

"Ah, Canon," she chided gently — and it struck him she might have been warned of such reactions on his part — "There's no need at all for crying. It will do you no good at all."

Her voice struck him as remote and it seemed she was addressing a stranger with the presumptiuious familiarity pity evokes.

"Sit up, Canon, and have the bit of breakfast. Doctor Barrett says you have to eat even if it's only a bit of porridge or a slice of buttered toast." She slid a hand behind his back and with a strength and deftness which surprised him, she eased him forward and shaking out the pillows behind, she slipped a bolster under them to prop up his body. Had he wished, he could not now sneak back into that warm and dreamless sleep he found so alluring. She tied a napkin about his neck and spread a bath towel across his knees. She spoonfed him some porridge which was weak and much too sweet. He grimaced in distaste and almost snarled at his lack of strength and vitality and at his complete humiliation in being hand fed. She pressed the metal rim of the spoon against his closed lips and in turn against his teeth which he held tightly clamped shut. She persisted and yielding he swallowed some more of the mush which fortunately was luke-warm rather than piping hot. It went down without much difficulty but Mrs O'Sullivan insisted that he drink some milk from a tumbler after each spoonful. He was hardly aware that she was sitting on the edge of the bed. He was ravenously hungry. He ate avidly, much to Mrs O'Sullivan's delight; she beamed at him as she muttered appreciation and words of encouragement, much as one would do to a recalcitrant toddler. "That's great, Canon. That's great altogether." He signalled that he had swallowed sufficient but was ignored. "A few more spoonfuls and then I have the lovely poached egg and a slice of buttered toast for you." He was hardly in a position to object. He detested the whole ritual. The sight of others being fed revolted him and never failed to conjure up childhood memories of birds feeding worms to their young. The long, pink earthworm being insinuated into the gaping mouth of a nestful of newly hatched fledglings with insatiable appetites. He dismissed the image and struggled with the poached egg which she offered. He then nibbled the toast between sips of tea from a mug which was held to his lips. The tea was strong, well sweetened and he was soothed at the simple but considerable comfort it gave him. Mrs O'Sullivan was well pleased with her morning's work. She wiped his chin and gently dabbed at his mouth with a damp cloth. "You're great. Great altogether. You wouldn't care for another mug of tea?" He shook his head emphatically. "Would you care for a smoke maybe?" He was severely tempted but thought it too imtimate an act to share with his housekeeper. He again shook his head. Mrs O'Sullivan smiled complacently, rose to her feet and gathered on a tray all the breakfast ware. Then as she was about to leave she turned towards him and her voice less certain and controlled than previously, she asked, "Do you want to evacuate your bowels, or relieve yourself in any way?"

Dumbfounded he gazed at her. She mistook his look for one of confusion. She repeated the question. He glared at her in unmistakable anger. She flushed but did not give up, nor did she discard the newly acquired air of familiarity he was finding so intolerable. "Doctor Barrett said to be sure and ask you," she said lightly by way of explanation. "I'm leaving this shoe by your bed and if you want anything Canon, anything," she repeated in emphasis, "just hit it off the floor. One of us is bound to hear you." She paused and pursed her lips. She retraced her steps and laid the tray on the bed. "Oh, I nearly forgot. The doctor left me some tablets. You're to take one three times a day." She fumbled about in her smock and took out among other things a small pill box. She opened it carefully and took out a white pill. She offered it to him with a glass of water. "Just swallow that and I'll leave you in peace till dinner time at least." He tried to resist. His emotions were not as controlled as he would wish them to be. He had no desire to give vent to his fury or aggravate the situation. He took the pill and swallowed it with a sip of water. Mrs O'Sullivan stood and regarded him, he thought, like someone overlooking an enemy fallen in battle after close combat: the victor was taking the measure of her now powerless opponent. He thought he would have to assert his authority strongly once his slight indisposition was past. Unbidden, she strode across the room and pulled the blinds half way down the windows. "The glare is terrible hard on the eyes and the sun will be streaming through in no time at all. You'd be baked alive." She took up the tray and left.

He lay quite still. By his bedside Bran lay stretched, his tongue protruding, his flanks rising and falling steadily. The presence of his dog was companionable. He could not see the clock nor judge the time from the sunlight in the garden. He estimated it was about eleven and felt anger that Father Phelan had not appeared following his summons. He dozed and eventually drifted into sleep. He woke suddenly to find sun streaming through the lower halves of the windows. He caught distant but distinct laughter. All three — his housekeeper and two curates — were sharing a joke. Father Good's snigger was high and brittle, reedy, Father Phelan gave a full and rotund guffaw and Mrs O'Sullivan was as near complete mirth as he had ever heard her approach. Their gaiety had a carefree quality he had never heard before within the Parochial House in all the years he had lived there. When the cat's away the mice will play, he thought grimly and not without some envy. The chuckles ceased abruptly and then silence settled. He longed to summon Father Phelan and enquire indirectly who had ministered to the Madden girl during his illness, but he knew Father Phelan to be too wise a bird for that. Disconsolate, he decided to bide his time and raise the question as inconsequently as possible. Sighing, he drifted into sleep, gladly delivering himself to the narcotic effects of the pill he had taken.

When he woke some time later he was instantly aware that he was not alone. He tried to focus his eyes but failed for a few moments. Father Phelan was standing by the bed. Bran was licking his hand affectionately and the priest was scratching him absently behind the ear. He looked at the Canon as though seeing him for the first time. He in turn noted instantly that the curate was more presentable in dress and appearance than was usually the case. His hair had been cut very recently. He had shaved more carefully than was his habit. The man obviously had not been drinking for some time. He continued to gaze at his superior in the bed much as Mrs O'Sullivan had. The mighty fallen, he thought glumly, to the immeasurable delight of the low.

Father Phelan spoke. "How are you, Canon?" He was offended by the quite self-assurance of the man slightly more than he resented his presence. He also smouldered at the helplessness in which he now found himself. He shut his eyes and asked tiredly, "Is there anything you wish to say, Father Phelan?"

"I am delighted to see you looking so well." The remark was cynically made and not altogether without some insolence.

"Thank you, Father. That is very kind of you. Was there anything else?"

"Mrs Ellen O'Leary died. Her burial took place this morning."

He nodded to show that he had heard and understood. The woman had been in her eighties and very charitable when it came to supporting the Foreign Missions and other good causes. She was vicious and vindictive to those who worked for her, be they servant or labourer, man or woman. She was frequently unjust to them and those over whom she held any sway. She was without consideration in dealing with others. She also paid handsome dues at Christmas and Easter but he, for his part, refused to take any of her money nor would he accept donations made for his personal use. He felt no comment was called for upon her death. He made none.

"Was there anything else, Father?"

The curate shrugged. The man, his superior thought, radiated hatred and malice. "Mr Cunningham called about the repairs to the sacristy roof and the repair of the headstones damaged by vandals in the cemetery in the last few weeks." He paused, aware of the scowl on the Canon's face. "I authorised him to go ahead with the repairs to the headstones and surrounds. But I told him he would have to consult you personally before undertaking any work on the church building."

"Quite so," he murmured, at first bristling at the idea of Father

Phelan authorising even the repairs to the headstones but placated once he heard the priest had quite rightly deferred to him on restoration of the roof. He closed his eyes and drew breath steadily at measured intervals in an effort to quell a sense of rising panic. His heart was beating rapidly and he feared his tension would show. How, he wondered, could he broach the subject without displaying undue concern.

The quandry was resolved for him. Father Phelan spoke impersonally, professionally, and the Canon was aware that the man's eyes were on him as he continued to speak, watching for the slightest flicker of an eyelid or any sign of unusual interest on his part.

"I attended Miss Madden, Miss Catherine Madden of Copley's Lane, in her present illness."

He trembled as if subject to a bitter blast of wind. Catherine, he thought, I never asked her name . . . or perhaps I did and I failed to remember . . . Catherine, so beautiful, so evocative, so very memorable a name. How suitable it seemed.

"She received?" he asked falteringly.

"She received, Canon. Very devoutly indeed. Her parents asked for you and expressed concern on hearing of your indisposition. They also requested, very strongly, I must say, that you should resume attendance upon their daughter as soon as your health permits."

He thought of the weary wife who sobbed silently while he unwillingly took the meagre hospitality so unstintingly offered. The husband who maintained a calm exterior and whose eyes, and only his eyes, betrayed the anguish. Gratitude flooded his entire being with an intoxicating sense of the reviviscent.

"They said as much?"

The reply was strongly affirmative: "Yes, Canon. They did."

There was no mistaking the emphasis, the undoubted sincerity of the man's words. Misery overwhelmed and a sense of helplessness. I never gave them a crumb of comfort, he thought bitterly, self-accusative. I never in any way sought to lessen their sorrow in their hour of trial. How could they possibly express such wishes?

"And Miss Madden's health?"

"It continues to deteriorate, I regret to say."

The Canon feared he would whimper. "Is she in pain?"

"She is in some pain, Canon." Father Phelan's voice was above all blunt and pragmatic.

"She suffers then?"

"She suffers somewhat, Canon."

His emotions began to exert themselves, the sense of loss and desolation was painfully accrescent as was the strange desire of his soul to receive from the dying girl's suffering the great grace of renewed faith and belief in the tenuous presumption of a paradise to come.

He spoke through clenched teeth, his face contorted by pain, "Thank you, Father. You may go."

"There is nothing I can do for you?"

"Nothing whatever, thank you, Father Phelan."

Bran rose and stretched himself with luxurious ease. He then yelped sharply and squatting on his hind quarters, gazed expectantly at Father Phelan.

"You don't mind if I take Bran for a run? It seems as though he could do with one."

"Please do so. I would be most grateful."

Father Phelan left, Bran trotting excitedly by his side. He heard the dog tumble down the stairs and felt a twinge of jealousy as he always did whenever the setter showed attachment to anyone but himself. The hall door opened and closed. The dog's barks rang on the clear air of day. He imagined he heard the crunch of gravel underfoot as Father Phelan made his way down the drive to the poplar walk beyond the cemetery and the open green fields which lay beyond.

Unbroken silence descended upon the house. They expressed a wish that I should attend her in her last illness he thought. I who give her untransmuted bread and empty though sonorous cant. He found himself yearning that the Christ of his early years as a priest, whom he had adored and loved as the true centre existence, would come walk with him again, if only until such time as she was finally delivered from her suffering. He experienced once more that void as he had when he realised he no longer believed and he had lost his love, his haunting Christus. He released the turbulence he had so long suppressed and howled, drifting eventually into the refuge of sleep.

When he woke the upper half of his room was in shade, the lower part was flooded in bright sunshine. He felt his bowels begin to loosen. He tried to deny their urgency but failed. He hesitated, loath to lean out and strike the flood with the shoe as directed by Mrs O'Sullivan. Suddenly his bowels flowed. He smarted at the humiliation, the foul warmth about his buttocks. He lay as still as possible, his dismay and discomfort increasing with each passing moment. Eventually he conceded defeat and tried in vain to lean over the side of the bed intending to summon the housekeeper. He sank back in the bed, spreading the mess about his thin flanks. He groaned aloud, savage rage at the stupidity of the woman. If only she had put a bell on the bedside table within easy reach ... If only he himself had thought of a bell ... He lay quite still, the smell beginning to rise and permeate the air of the room. He tried to stifle it somewhat by holding his breath but found that made him dizzy and forced him to compensate by taking deep draughts of the fouled air. He listened attentively. Nothing stirred in the deeply tranquil house. It was not, he knew instinctively, empty. There was someone downstairs. Father Good or perhaps Mrs O'Sullivan. He did not particularly wish to summon either and let them know of his shame, still less have them help him. His anger kindled, he swelled with rage, his head throbbed painfully. Quite unexpectedly there was a tentative sound on the landing. He called out roughly to whoever it might be.

To his surprise Father Good entered, a breviary in his hand. He approached the bed cautiously and evidently soon sensed the foul air of the room. He flushed and stammered: "I found your breviary downstairs. I thought you might like to have it."

"Is Father Phelan in?" he demanded, ignoring the excuse.

"Yes, Canon. He is. He is just back from his afternoon walk."

"Send him to me ... Send him to me at once ... Don't just stand there gaping. Send the man to me at once!" He heard his own voice re-echo about the room, enraged and fraught with hysteria.

"Yes, Canon." Thoroughly abject Father Good stumbled away. He heard him hurry along the landing and descend the staircase. Silence ensued. An unnecessarily long silence, he thought. Then there was an urgent tap at the door and without waiting to be summoned, Father Phelan entered.

"You sent for me, Canon?"

They exchanged glances of rank hostility and he believed that the priest was not above relishing his humiliation. He had in his time subjected the man to not simply humiliation but debasement. What could he then expect? Plainly the man knew of his accident. It showed on his face for all that he tried to remain impassive. It showed more clearly in the eyes in a small but fulgent light and faintly on his curled lips. I have rarely done the decent thing with him, he thought. Why expect to receive what one had never given? He took a deep breath and succumbed as he knew Father Phelan wished him to do.

"I have soiled my bed, Father Phelan. Please be so good as to assist me. I am helpless and I do not wish Mrs O'Sullivan to see me in my present state. Now or later."

Father Phelan stood still. Stock still and stared frankly at him. For one moment he thought the man was going to refuse him aid. "Of course, Canon. If you suffer the discomforture for a little longer I will have some water heated and fetch a clean pair of sheets and pyjamas. Perhaps it would help if I opened the windows?" He nodded frantically in assent. Fresh air wafted into the room and blew all about him. He drew deep breath with something akin to gratitude. Father Phelan lingered rather than hastening about his task. He took a packet of cigarettes from his pocket, placed two between his lips and lit them. He inhaled.

"Doctor Barrett was here. You were asleep. He thought it best not to disturb you. He will be calling back later this afternoon or evening." He wished the man would hurry but instead he offered him a cigarette. "Have a smoke. It will relieve your tension."

The Canon glanced sharply at the heavy man in almost shapeless clerical clothing, searching for the subdued malice so easily recognisable in his eyes some seconds before. There was nothing there but kindness. Father Phelan held the cigarette to his lips and he drew hungrily on it. His head whirled as the smoke curled about his lungs but the sensation was pleasant. Father Phelan squatted by the bed and withdrew the cigarette from time to time, enabling him to inhale and exhale in comfort and derive the maximum from each puff. He thought it a generous act, the impulsive gesture of a soft-hearted person. He felt moved. Tears gathered in his eyes.

"It won't take long, Canon," the priest assured him softly. "And it will never happen again. The doctor has arranged for a nurse to attend you during the day at least."

He thought his condition hardly warranted a nurse but the presence of one would at least spare him the indignity of having others attend to his personal hygiene. Father Phelan took the cigarette stub from his mouth and stubbed it out on an ashtray on the mantlepiece.

"It won't take long, Canon, I assure you."

After his curate had left, he wondered how he could face the ordeal ahead. He had not been seen naked by anyone, other than his doctor, for over sixty years. Dislike of his body, which had none of the symmetry of John's, had been in him since very early childhood, unlovely and in a way he found inexplicable, unclean. The encounter with the sailor in the docklands area had reinforced the feeling. Religious instruction had further instilled this inhibition almost to self-detestation. He ruminated on the rather despoiled temple of the Holy Spirit which the human body was purported to be. He had seen them take John from the

Blackwater after a long day's search. He had been discovered
lightly entangled in river growths and when extracted from the
weeds, lovingly done by his grandfather, the body was quite
without mark or bruise of any kind, the eyes open, the face
perfectly calm and his skin had the remarkable uniform light tan
it never, even in winter, lost and had not yet acquired the pallor of
the dead. They laid him on a trestle in the boathouse and draped a
sheet about his lower torso. The body was wet and the sheet
adhered to the flesh, outlining his classical physique. It had been
difficult for him to accept that John was dead. Though some
twelve or fourteen years had separated them in age, John had
been his only companion and he had known nothing but
benevolence from him. In summer when at home from college he
had taught him to swim. He rarely returned from visits to the
homes of his friends without bringing some small gift to mark the
occasion. A few times he had taken him camping at Roches Point
or Rostellan. Somehow he had believed that at a certain age he
would cease to be gauche and emerge as physically striking as
John but he lacked John's basic sturdiness, his ruddy good
health, his stamina which made him so successful a competitor in
field events at the College and University. He, on the other hand,
was what was then referred to as 'a delicate child' and he had been
admitted to the seminary only on tolerance. Even then he had to
have a special dispensation allowing him to take his exams in
stages, rather than over a few days of concentrated labour as was
the case with all his fellow students. He slept in the sick bay during
that period, held incommunicado and under oath not to discuss
the exams or their subject matter with anyone. He had hoped that
with John dead his parents might lavish their love on him.
Through an oversight he had been present when his father having
travelled up from the city by the late train, had examined the body
of his dead son by the swaying light of a lantern. His grief had
been great and unmistakable, a sorrow largely of the eyes because
he had neither wept nor exclaimed nor showed any other sign of
loss or mourning. Watching from the periphery of the crowd
about the body he had on impulse stolen forward and slipped his
hand into that of his father. He had responded by squeezing it,
apparently in sympathy. Then, as if coming out of a reverie he
had turned and glared in hatred at his living son. Abruptly
dropping the boy's hand he wheeled and roughly pushed past
those who offered their condolences. Adulation for his father
suddenly gushed away as if from an open wound. His father's
dying words had been a plea for John. His mother had coped
with her grief by complete withdrawal from everyone about her,

confining herself to the house and refusing to receive all visitors, even the more immediate members of the family. Not until they were both dead had he realised that he had been emotionally disinherited from the day John had died.

He was incapable of love and sensuality aroused in him only disgust. Assertions of the flesh therefore had never caused him any difficulty.

Father Phelan attended to him discreetly. He changed his linen, washed his soiled body with surprising tenderness for so big a man and gave him a clean night shirt.

Shortly after he had eaten a huge meal which Mrs O'Sullivan insisted on referring to as his 'tea', Doctor Barrett arrived. He looked with dislike at the physician. "I would have imagined that even an oaf of the lowest kind would have thought fit to make provision for my hygiene and not compel dependence on those beneath me to deal with my intimate needs." The rancour in his voice was undisguised. He directed it as one would a honed spear or some similar weapon in the hope of wounding.

Doctor Barrett was quite unimpressed. He blinked rapidly for some seconds and looked at the Canon intently as if he were a mildly interesting biological specimen of which he had heard but not seen before. "Of course, but you must appreciate this is a small provincial town. Arranging for a good, efficient nurse with wide experience is not as readily done as in a large city. So I am very fortunate indeed to have acquired the services of Mrs Horan who held a responsible position in a London hospital before returning to marry."

"Is she qualified?"

"Fully qualified, I assure you. Now I have to take your pulse. Please let me have your hand."

The Canon did not comply. "You were directly responsible for the most bitter humiliation I have ever had to suffer. Due solely to your lack of foresight I soiled the bed and myself and had to endure the ignobility of being cleaned up by one of my priests."

"Then all I can say is that you were very well looked after indeed. As for humiliation and ignobility, as you who administer to the sick and aged well know, many, many worthy people, with a sense of bodily integrity as acute and as sensitive as yours, have not only to undergo such so called degradation every day but have to do so in considerable agony in some cases. And do so without complaint. You hand, Canon. I wish to take your pulse." The voice was commanding.

"I cannot raise my arm. I am without the use of my limbs. I seem to have weakened considerably."

"Thank you, Canon. That is all I wanted to know." Doctor Barrett grasped his wrist and felt his pulse. His fingers were short and stubby, well fleshed and warm. Why not, he thought savagely. The man is a medic. He battens on suffering. His big, protruding gut testifies to his insatiable gluttony. Barrett withdrew his hand. he reached inside his jacket for a folded handkerchief. He shook it loose and it spilled open, its brilliant white catching the reflected light of evening. He took off his glasses and began to wipe them while blinking myopically at some of the now indistinct objects in the room. The figure on the bed he ignored.

"How long must I remain before you condescend to speak to me?" He felt his jaw slacken, his lips quiver. Darkness again threatened.

The doctor addressed him. "I am not at all pleased with your progress. It is my considered opinion that you should be transferred to some nursing home, in town if necessary but preferably one by the sea. Saint Michael's at Kilbrittin perhaps."

"Has it occurred to you that I am charged with the responsibilities in this parish and cannot lightly rid myself of these?"

"I am perfectly aware of that, Canon, but you have a duty to yourself and to your parish to see that you are in good health to discharge those commitments more faithfully." He ground his teeth when he spat, "I am not ill."

"You are ill, Canon." The retort was sharp and quick in coming. "You are suffering from nervous prostration. Now you either remain here and accept fully the limitations I will put upon your actions or I will have no alternative but to transfer you to a properly appointed nursing home. To do less would be dereliction of my duty as your physician."

He pondered for seconds. The threat in Barrett's tone was clear. If forced to, he would carry out his duty as he saw it. "How long will I be like this?"

"Impossible to say." Doctor Barrett sounded mollified to some degree. "A few weeks perhaps at the outmost, provided you follow my instructions and do not tax yourself unduly. You are exceeding yourself and have been for some time. If you fail to rest now and recuperate you might well suffer a complete nervous breakdown compounded by physical collapse. It might render you unfit for parish duties of any kind for the rest of your life." Barrett shot the priest a sharp glance. Incidental light danced on the surface of the doctor's glasses. "I must make it clear. Either you place yourself completely in my hands and obey or I will refuse to be responsible for you. You must consent to my treatment. Do I have that consent, Canon?" Barrett paused and looked grimly at him.

He considered for some seconds and then nodded weakly. "Yes, Doctor, you have my agreement. My full agreement," he added for emphasis.

The physician exhaled slowly. "Good! I will give you something to relax you. Not a sleeping draught as such, though it might well help you sleep more restfully. Mrs Horan, that is the former Sister Horan, will be on duty first thing in the morning. She is altogether an admirable person and ideally suited to supervise your treatment. As I said, she held a most responsible position in one of London's finest teaching hospitals. She will attend to your comfort and wellbeing at all times and if by chance you do suffer an accidental call of nature, something which for reasons I personally cannot understand you consider degrading, Father Phelan can summon her quickly as she lives in Crowley's Road not five minutes from here. Effectively she will be at your call twenty-four hours, day and night."

"How do I summon the good lady? You present me with a brass lamp which I rub and lo, the woman materialises before my very eyes!" The sarcasm in his voice was splenetic. He almost exhulted in it.

Barrett frowned. "Totally uncalled for and most unworthy. The good woman is merely obliging me, as she has in the past, by consenting to attend to you. She already has the responsibility of four children and the financial rewards from her spell of duty are hardly likely to be great."

He sighed. A silence ensued during which Barrett fiddled with his bag and its contents. "My apologies. It was as you say, most unworthy. What I meant to ask was how do I summon anyone to my room. I had thought of a bell but it is doubtful if anyone would hear a bell, even in the dead of night."

"Thank you, Canon. I accept your apologies. I will speak to Father Phelan about the matter. It should take a competent electrician less than ten minutes to attach an electric buzzer to the wall by your bed, run a wire through the floorboards to the kitchen downstairs and an extension to Father Phelan's bedroom. If a mishap should occur, day or night, you can summon Father Phelan who will in turn fetch Mrs Horan. Meanwhile I will have your housekeeper position a bell by your bed. I take it there is a bell in the house?"

There was. The high-toned brass bell which he used to summon Mrs O'Sullivan from the kitchen between courses. It would hardly be heard at any great distance but it would do for the moment.

The doctor snapped his bag shut firmly. "Remember, I expect my directions to be carried out to the letter. Otherwise I will refuse all responsibility for you and leave your health in the hands of whoever you choose to trust." He nodded tiredly. "Good evening, Canon. Sleep well."

"Could I have a few words, Doctor, ..." His voice trailed off hesitantly. The doctor turned towards him attentively. "About Miss Madden — of Copley's Lane. You are attending her?"

"Yes. I am attending her."

"Forgive me for asking, but I am attending to her spiritually in her illness. I would like to know if it in no way involves a breach of confidence, whether she will suffer a great deal?"

The physician again blinked disconcertingly and paused before responding. "No, I do not think replying to your question would in any way involve a breach of confidence. Her heart is strong, unhappily in this instance. She is also a young lady of remarkable strength of mind. If her heart were less sturdy it might weaken and eventually release her from her misery. If the will to live were less strong, she might, just might, succumb before her illness enters its final stages. Since such is not the case, I fear she will linger on and suffer accordingly."

"Are there not drugs available which might alleviate her pain?"

"Some. But they are available only in small quantities and are not as effective as the opiates available before the outbreak of war."

"Forgive me. I have no intention of imputing your undoubtedly justified reputation as above all a compassionate as well as a competent man — but — it is not a question of payment?"

He heard the sharp intake of breath which sounded like the hiss of a coiled and hidden serpent. "I assure you, Canon, it is not a matter of payment. Effective opiates are simply not available."

He stared at the figure now looming large over him in the rapidly darkening room. "You will do everything to relieve her pain?"

"Yes. I will."

"Thank you. Thank you." He heard the words which were heavily charged with emotion and were spoken with a sincerity he could scarcely credit himself capable of feeling. He had rarely used them other than as a shoddy social necessity.

The physician approached his bed. "Canon," he began uncertainly, "I want you to do something for me. I want you to oblige me by no longer visiting Miss Madden."

He heard the words so clearly enunciated. He had anticipated them the moment the doctor had begun to speak. "Why do you ask that of me?"

"For your own sake. For your continued good health and wellbeing. I fear your health might suffer irrepairably if you continue to attend her."

"Thank you, Doctor Barrett, that is very considerate of you but I have an obligation and whatever the price I may have to pay, I shall continue to do my duty as I see it."

"Nothing then I may say will alter your decision?"

"Nothing whatever. Nothing whatever."

"Very well. You do your duty as you see fit and I shall do mine. Goodnight."

He responded to the doctor's farewell but so faintly it was lost.

He woke during the night feeling a slight chill penetrate the room. Father Phelan in his dressing gown, an old overcoat slung loosely over his shoulders and a blanket over his knees was smoking furtively, the cigarette cupped in his hand, the nearby bedroom window open slightly at the bottom to prevent stuffiness. His first reaction was one of irritation, then gratitude overcame him. Secure, he slept soundly and at dawn Father Phelan had gone. He felt he was surfacing to a new day, a new beginning such as the young are apt to feel in the first flush of their untempered exuberance.

6

He entered the sanctuary followed by his server, the sacristan Mr Duran. He genuflected and mounted the steps to the altar where he placed the chalice and its covering veil before the tabernacle. He felt weak and unsteady on his feet but determined nevertheless to resume his duties. Retracing his steps, he descended to the foot of the altar and blessing himself in broad strokes chanted softly "Introibo ad altare Dei", to which Duran responded even more softly "Ad deum qui laetificat juventutem meum". He intoned the opening phrases of the prescribed psalm and suddenly he experienced joy. He felt once more the palpable presence of God in the tabernacle on the altar before him, in the church itself, and in his heart. It flooded him and he was grateful. He praised her, the simple young woman whom he believed to be the vessel from which this grace in abundance was showered upon him.

Now his movements were infused with profound significance quite beyond the ability of even the most intent observer to perceive, still less comprehend. His frail, unlovely body spanned the centuries involved as if for the first time in the slaughter of the Christ. Paradoxically with joy came grief. Grief at the tremendous moment fast approaching when Christ would become a living presence in his hands and would once more suffer the agony on the cross with a renewed sorrow at the vast number of souls who would refuse the dearly bought means of salvation. He would stand by Him again — the joyous companion of his early manhood — the Christ beloved of John and Peter and Paul, of the other faithful disciples, of all the saints whose number were vast and of many, many millions who had trod this earth since last He bowed His head, since the cry "Consumatum Est" was wrung from His heart and ripped from His lips. He felt the immense suffering of the Divine Heart and was swept by desolation and yet he did not despair. From the spilled blood, he knew, many graces would blossom and the earth and all mankind, particularly those who sickened or suffered in any way would be instantly renewed. He was an instrument of grace and had therefore to pay the price for such an exalted privilege in ultimate exile, sundered from the world of the flesh and the material that he might be all the more singular a servant of the Lord.

Father Phelan glanced at him as he passed by to a side altar on the left of the sanctuary. He genuflected and saw the Canon rapt and intent upon his prayers. He could not fail but be struck by his devotion, his attentiveness and most noticeably, a humility not hitherto remarkable in a man whom he considered arrogant and proud.

The parish priest held high the consecrated bread and without reservation, adored it. He raised up the blood in its chalice of gold and it also he adored. Later he descended to the altar rails and with a great sense of destiny he distributed the hosts to those who hungered for them. He prayed that their hunger might be satisfied and that they might now know abiding grace for their heroic devotion to the mass and all it represented.

Later he was amicable at breakfast, or at least he thought of himself as being amicable, though he did notice a sardonic grin on Father Phelan's face during an unguarded moment. After breakfast he strolled in the garden and read the Divine Office and again he was infused with a sense of wonder and awe. He said the prayers as if discovering their potency for the first time. He read them heartfully and felt they soared as might a song to the very throne of God. He was, he realised, happy, immeasurably so, and was duly grateful.

He panicked as he approached her house having run the gauntlet of Whelan crouched behind his half-door, his mangy mongrel for once confined within. He found it difficult to analyse his fear. Was it, he wondered, a fear that she might die during the hours of darkness when he would not be there to administer extreme unction and pronounce the absolution for the dying? Surely nothing could be so grossly selfish, nothing so nakedly egotistical. That she might slip into a coma or be in such pain that she might not recognise him? Yes, he admitted reluctantly, that would be a great sorrow to him but he was at least aware of the danger.

He pushed in the wooden garden gates which had been newly painted. The main door had also been painted a lighter shade of blue and the garden, with its perennial flowers in full flush, showed careful attention. He had scarcely reached the door when it was opened without having to knock.

He entered and sensed fear. An atavistic fear of startling power and potency. A coldness gripped his heart as he sought to examine the eyes of Madden and his wife. They failed to meet his eye and the coldness passed as quickly and as inexplicably as it had come. He felt sufficiently strong to deal with anything. The woman rose and carefully positioning her candle in a holder on the table, she took his greatcoat and his biretta, his scarf and his gloves. Though it was a day of soft sunshine and quite warm, he had found that since his minor relapse he experienced extremes of temperature to an extraordinary degree. He signalled his readiness to go upstairs. She preceded him up the staircase to the bedroom. On entering he noticed a bower of blue and white paper flowers under which stood a statue of the Blessed Virgin and at its feet a profusion of flowers. Instinctively he realised it was her childhood altar remade most likely by her father. In her last days they wished her to be consoled by its presence.

He detected the faintest flicker of an eyelash. Her eyes were glittering, quite the most intense he had ever seen. They seemed to radiate sharp light from some inner source. They were strikingly beautiful as were her facial features though she was clearly marked for death and her skin had taken on the hue of pale beaten bronze. Her eyelids again moved. She smiled slightly and gazed at him directly for some seconds. As though that was far too tasking, she closed her eyes and sank into a state of serene, soul-affecting repose. His heart thumped within the confines of his chest, his blood scorched. She had undoubtedly recognised him.

He lay the pyx on the table with its lighted candles and two small cut glass cases filled with lily-of-the-valley. He took his stole from his jacket pocket, kissed it and draping it about his neck indicated to the parents that they should now withdraw. They did so silently, swiftly. He was aware of a fresh breeze blowing through the room, though no window was open despite the heat of the day, scented with fresh flowers and sweet foliage.

He knelt to hear her confession. The effort proved too much for her. He bade her softly to be silent and to conserve her strength. He asked her to consider with him as consciously as she could the five wounds of Christ and what might be their significance in terms of this world and in the life of the immemorial soul. He named the wounds and equating them with the five human senses, entered into deep meditation with her. Concluding, he was drawn irresistibly towards her. Gently, with infinite care he raised her upper body and held her in his arms in a loose embrace. He held her tenderly, conscious of her womanliness, her unbelievable fragility, her soft, human warmth. Worldlessly they communed and he was enraptured. From time to time she whimpered in pain. Her body shot taut and rigid. She cried out but almost inaudibly. He willed with all his being that by some great dispensation she might draw comfort and fortitude from his unworthy caress.

Mrs Madden called quietly, "Canon, Canon." The angelus bell rang in the distance. The air absorbed its sound. Reduced, it sounded as from a great way off, another world. He gently eased her back onto the bed, resting her head on the pillow and resisting the temptation to stroke her hair or kiss her on the brow, he imparted absolution and gave her the sacrament. They remained in prayer for some further time and then, quenching the candles, he returned the pyx to its position inside his jacket and taking the stole from about his shoulders, he kissed it and carefully folded it. He longed inexpressibly to remain with her through all her days and nights of suffering but knew he could not.

The table was laid as usual when he went downstairs, the woman hovering about anxiously, the teapot on the table. The man was sitting on a chair, his legs spread wide, his hands resting on his thighs. His teeth were clenched about the stem of his pipe but the pipe was unlit. The woman smiled as she poured his tea but it was not a genuine smile. Her eyes remained solemn, clouded by fear. He sipped his tea in silence for some time and munched a biscuit self-consciously, as he always ate in the houses of others. He looked at the man.

"Please feel free to smoke your pipe if you wish. It will not disturb me in any way."

Both men exchanged glances and Madden took a handkerchief from his pocket and furtively wiped his lips.

"Is there perhaps something you wish to tell me? Something you think I should know?"

The woman's hand shot to her mouth as if to stifle a cry. She burst into tears and sat in one of the kitchen chairs by the fireside. She moaned and drew breath with difficulty. The sounds were uncomfortably like those of a death rattle.

"It's alright, Canon," the man assured him. "She's a bit upset."

"Perhaps if I were to leave," he ventured half-rising from the table.

"No, Canon, no . . . There's something we don't understand, . . . something we need to ask you about."

"If I can help in any way." He tried to sound sympathetic and approachable.

The man had taken the pipe from his mouth and was now examining it with all the care of an intending purchaser feigning casualness. He reached a hand towards the woman. She grabbed it frantically and held tightly, desperately, still weeping. The man tried to speak but faltered. He licked his lips nervously and tried again. "Something has been happening, Canon ... to Catherine ... It's happened a few times now .. at night ... a light, ... a very bright light has appeared in her room ... and she's been speaking to someone. ... Wide awake and alert ... as she used to be before she was taken sick. Talking, speaking. Very plainly. Like she was talking to a friend."

He contemplated the man. He was a practical, straightforward person from what he knew of him. Not at all the sort to be easily frightened and certainly not the type to resort to deceit or succumb to hysteria. There followed a long pause.

"A light," he said. "What kind of light?"

"Blue-green". The man gestured helplessly. "Then it turned white. Very white. Brilliant. Like the sun."

"Did the light emanate from any particular source?"

The man hesitated.

"Did the light come from any particular thing or part of the room?"

The man shook his head. "It was just there. In her bedroom. I walked through it." He again paused and his wife's hand tightened about his. "I cast no shadow when I walked through that light, Canon."

He concentrated on what he had heard. In popular mythology demons taking human form cast no shadow. He was not unduly disturbed. The room after all did have a skylight and day or night, light could play tricks. It needed just a little imagination to turn the rational and easily explicable into the mysterious and unknown. He himself had sensed no evil in the young woman or in the room. On the contrary, he had the distinct and ever increasing impression that grace and simple goodness was present in abundance.

"You say she was speaking. What was she saying?"

"I couldn't make it out. She spoke clearly but I couldn't understand. It was like she was speaking another language."

"Her voice was strong and firm and she spoke with clarity yet you couldn't understand what was being said."

"Yes. That's it."

"Was she happy?"

"Yes," he nodded emphatically, "she was very happy." The man may not have realised it but there was gratitude in his voice.

The priest gazed at the unlit fire in the range, its bundled paper, its crossed kindling, its few sods of peat. It was past midday and he wondered why they had not lit the range to cook their afternoon meal. He thought of the young woman. Of how he had held her. Her warmth. Her femininity. The vivid impression of a fresh breeze blowing through the room, faint and beautifully scented. She was goodness, he thought, she was grace. There was nothing tainted or evil about her.

"You have discussed this with no one?"

The couple exchanged glances. The man replied: "We called one of the neighbours. Mrs O'Dowd from further up the street. She sometimes calls to see Catherine, to bring a small gift or just to sit and keep her company."

"Mrs Eileen O'Dowd?"

The man nodded.

He knew the woman, though not very well. Rich, as wealth would be calculated in any provincial town. Comfortable might be a more exact phrase. A woman of charity in all things and a woman of good works. A daily communicant. Her only son, a very promising student by reputation was serving with the British Royal Air Force. his father, also an aviator, had been killed during the Great War. His body has never been discovered. She had a special mass said for the repose of his soul on each November eleventh. She drew her blinds on that day and in her manner kept it holy, refusing to meet any callers or undertake any business or social commitments. She would, he thought, be sufficiently courageous to face the unknown, particularly if by doing so she could allay the fears of those who had already suffered a great deal. More importantly, she could be relied upon not to gossip.

"What did she say?"

"She said it was something beautiful. Something holy, something to be grateful for."

He nodded and reasoned further with himself. From what he knew of Mrs O'Dowd she would not easily be duped and the parents themselves he believed were incapable of subterfuge of any kind, but then hysteria was an extraordinary phenomenon. There had been the case of the young Leeson girl in the city many years ago who had claimed to have seen the virgin and had infected the entire neighbourhood with her hallucinations. He remembered the poor, aged women with all their children in tattered clothes grasping the fringes of their shawls while they prayed before the gable end of a crumbling hovel in the Shannon Street area, then the poorest part of the city before development in the thirties had levelled the notorious slumland. They had held lighted candles in their hands. Some sang the Lourdes hymn and others chanted the rosary in a frenetic spate of words as possessed they swayed to and fro, some frothing from the mouth. The girl was shown up to be a liar, a poor innocent fantast who had later taken up with a soldier stationed in the town and had become pregnant; had to leave for England, never to be heard of again. He must prevent a re-occurrence if only because — besides being unseemly in the extreme — such affairs if not destructive of faith, cheapened it. And what was devalued he believed, was diminished forever.

He would have a word with Mrs O'Dowd. She at least could be relied upon to use her discretion and not spread the entire affair over town. As to the authenticity of the story he had heard, he had no doubt that the man believed in what he said. Mrs O'Dowd's version would, he felt, confirm that. He thought the incident — and that is how he thought of it — something to be dealt with soberly and endured for the sake of the dying girl.

"I must pledge you both to secrecy," he said, rising. "You must speak of these events to no one, not even Mrs O'Dowd, nor indeed to my priests. If there are any further ..." he paused seeking the right word, "developments, send for me personally. Is all that clearly understood?" He was at his commanding best and knew as much.

The man and woman nodded their heads.

He eyed them sternly. "How often has this happened before and why did you not send for Father Phelan or Father Good?"

The man flushed. The woman squeezed so tightly on his hand, her knuckles went white. She bared her teeth in an effort to control her emotions. "It happened twice before, Father. The first time we saw it we thought we were seeing things. That was a Monday night. Then it happened a second time on a Wednesday night ... We didn't feel ... didn't feel we could tell Father Phelan or Father Good."

"Why not?" He raised an eyebrow. "Why ever not? They are both God's anointed priests, priests of this parish."

The man again scrutinised his pipe. "We thought it best to wait for you, Canon."

"And if I had not come?"

"We knew you would. You gave your word. We know you are a man of your word."

Vanity asserted itself. He suppressed it firmly but only after some seconds of self-indulgence. "I see. If this happens again I wish to be informed immediately, irrespective of the hour of day or night. Mrs O'Dowd I believe has a telephone. I will arrange with her to call me at the Parochial House if you contact her. I will come instantly, but in the meanwhile I again pledge you to holy silence. Not a word of this to anyone."

They agreed and the woman helped him into his coat.

"Canon, you don't think this is . . . bad? The work of the . . ."

"No," he hastened to interrupt her before she could finish what she intended saying. "No! Most certainly not. This is the hand of God, not an abomination of Satan the prince of darkness. This may well be a great grace. Pray. Pray constantly that God might seek fit to have it so."

He left abruptly. He called upon Mrs O'Dowd who received him graciously in her drawing room, seated like a dowager queen on the edge of an antique gilt chair which looked uncommonly frail and insubstantial. She was a remarkably well preserved woman of perhaps sixty-five or so. Her hair was uniformly grey. Dyed he suspected, expensively and artfully to very good effect. Her eyes were intelligent and hinted a good sense of humour. She succinctly and unemotionally recounted her experience at the Maddens some nights previously.

Knowing the answer before he even posed the question, he asked: "Were you not afraid, Mrs O'Dowd?"

"No. Not at all. A bit apprehensive when I was asked by Mr Madden to go and witness this mysterious light he kept referring to. I simply did not know what to expect. But once I was there, once I was in the room, all apprehension vanished. I was struck, almost awed, by the great beauty of it all and what I took to be the presence of God."

He glanced sharply at her. She had not spoken carelessly. Her words he believed were scrupulously weighed at all times. Slipshod speech would hardly be characteristic of her. She met his glance unflinchingly.

"What did you do?"

"I knelt and prayed."

"And the Maddens?"

"They were terrified but then they too knelt and prayed."

"Following your example?"

"Possibly. Quite possibly, though I must admit I knelt not to set an example, but instinctively."

He reflected. "Why did you kneel? To pray?"

She touched the single strand of pearls about her neck. Even in the dim light of the room with its blind partially drawn as a protection against the sunlight, their creamy lustre was visible marking them as genuine and valuable, as did the blue glints of the diamonds on the brooch she wore on her dress above the right breast. Darting like subdued starlight, they showed the true nature of the stones. Her eyes hesitated on the silver-framed photograph of a young man in Royal Air Force uniform, but whether it was of her husband or son he could not tell from where he sat. She seemed perplexed. She blinked rapidly and in succession for some seconds. "How very strange that you ask that, Canon. Come to think of it, I knelt unhesitatingly in adoration."

He gasped faintly and looked at her in amazement. "Was there anyone or anything to adore, Mrs O'Dowd?"

"No. No, there was not. There was only this radiant light somewhere at the left and towards the end of the bed. I assumed there was someone there in human form because the girl was conversing happily with whomever or whatever it was. She was remarkably happy. Joyous. All sign of suffering had vanished and she was more beautiful than when she had her health. It was moving and I suppose a bit terrible."

An odd choice of word, he thought, to describe that which was possibly sanctified, terrible. Yet it was a term which cropped up time and time again in the writings and recollections of mystics even so recently as the last years of the century in the writings of Theresa of Lisieux. "Terrible?" he asked lightly.

"Yes. Awesome would not quite describe what I mean."

"You experienced no fear, no sense of evil, of the corrupt or tainted?"

The woman faced him directly, her green eyes mellowing with frankness. The hand was raised and she toyed absently with the pearls at her throat. "No, Canon. No sense of fear. No sense of evil or corruption. Quite the opposite, in fact. Holy joy and the tremendous urge to kneel and adore."

The assertion of authority in her statement and the manner in which it was made placed her sincerity beyond dispute. "You would be prepared to swear on sacred oath that all you have told me is the truth as you know it?"

"Yes, Canon," she replied briskly. "I would, and without reservation of any kind."

The clock on the mantlepiece chimed musically as if constructed to record only the happy passage of golden hours. He waited until the chimes had ceased and their echoes had died away in the still brightness of the room.

"Why did you not confide in me or one of my priests as to what you were being called upon to witness?"

"Oh, I thought of that, but I had given an undertaking to the Maddens not to discuss the matter with anyone." She said Maddens each time, he noted, not Mr and Mrs Madden but 'Maddens'. Her sense of class was as well defined as her code of behaviour. "I thought it possible however that a time might come when I would need to tell someone, in which case I had made up my mind to confide in Father Good, under the seal of confession."

"I see. Thank you Mrs O'Dowd. You have been most helpful. More so than I can say." He hesitated. "If you will forgive me, I gave the Maddens instructions to summon me through you if this incident should occur again. I hope you do not mind what I now realise was a presumption on my part?"

The gracious smile, the dismissive gesture of the right hand. "Of course not, Father. I cannot think of who else they could turn to. You were perfectly right to do as you did." He rose to his feet. She did likewise.

"Surely you are not leaving without some refreshment. Some tea perhaps?"

"Thank you, no. It will soon be time for my midday meal and I have already taken tea with the Maddens." He followed her to the door. In the hallway he paused and asked, "Do you know the Maddens well, Mrs O'Dowd?"

"Quite well," she replied. "Mrs Madden sometimes helped with preserving fruit and other food. I harvest all the fruit and vegetables and preserve what I possibly can. She used to do the cooking in the days when I was a little more socially active than I am now. She also washed and sewed for me. I entrusted all my old linen and laces to her. I still do. She washes them with great care and repairs them beautifully. She has extraordinarily gifted hands. And of course Catherine came and helped her mother from time to time. I know her as a vivacious child, not pretty but by no means plain or common. And Mr Madden. He does the garden whenever I let it get out of hand, which I seem to do nowadays with increasing frequency."

"Thank you for being so kind as to see me and for your frankness in answering all my questions. I am very much obliged."

"No at all, Canon. You are always most welcome."

A smile, he nodded and the door was silently shut behind him. He was struck by the fact that he had been in the presence of someone who knew how to keep people in their place — Canons not excepted. Her frank account of events he found disturbing. Her evidence if ever required would be very difficult to refute. He had been quietly hoping that the entire affair had been nothing but a form of collective delusion due to the intense strain the Maddens were under. At that it would have been understandable. Now however it had taken on a quite different dimension, one he would have preferred it had not. He spoke briefly with Father Phelan on his return to the Parochial House and questioned him obliquely about the visits he had made to the Madden household. Other than he had been greatly impressed by the girl's piety, Father Phelan had nothing to contribute. Somewhat curtly he brought the conversation to an end and dismissed the priest.

He sank into the fireside chair in his bedroom, feeling exhausted. He found himself confounded and he had not the vaguest idea of how best to proceed. He considered briefly reporting the matter to the Bishop but that was a dangerous course and though it might come to that in time, at present it would only give rise to untold complications. He half-prayed, half-hoped that the young girl would die fortified by the last rites of the church, in her sleep and so attain, if not endless happiness, release from suffering. He reached for his breviary intending to pray but found himself so overwhelmed by weariness, he dozed for a short time. On rousing he took a short walk with Bran. Afterwards he retired early. It was Tuesday, he reminded himself. He found himself thinking that the visions had taken place on Monday and Wednesday nights. He could therefore expect nothing that night. He was undisturbed and slept deeply as he did to his surprise the following night. He thought of calling to the Maddens to enquire if a visitation had in fact taken place but knew at once that such a course would be unwise.

He said his morning mass. All was empty ritual devoid of meaning, the joy central to the priesthood and which he had so happily regained, was totally absent. He discharged his duties for the day as best he could. At all meals he felt no desire whatever to speak, thus imposing silence upon those who dined with him. He again retired early and slipped easily into sleep. So conscious was he of someone's presence in his dreams that he called out softly, "Who is there?" He became aware of a soft, warm breeze, fragrant and fresh. He drew a short, sharp breath. The visitation he knew was taking place. He stumbled out of bed and slipped on his dressing gown. The telephone should ring at any moment. He did not want all those in the house alerted. He smoked a cigarette for some seconds but deriving no pleasure from the act, he stubbed it out impatiently. Waiting. Expectant. He washed in the cold water on the wash-stand and dressed properly. He heard the phone ring with shrill urgency.

He slipped downstairs and lifted the receiver off the hook. He whispered. The voice on the phone was as brisk and as confident as ever: "Mrs O'Dowd here, Canon. I'm telephoning to let you know that Mr Madden has been to see me and would like you to call on them if at all possible." He muttered his thanks somewhat furtively. Mrs O'Dowd bade him good-night crisply and the line went dead. Mrs O'Sullivan and Father Phelan were both on the landing. Father Phelan spoke with some concern.

"Is it a sick-call, Canon? Perhaps you would like me to go?"

"It is from the Maddens." He felt he had to be as truthful as possible. "It is not a sick-call as such but they wish to see me urgently. I must go." The couple on the landing exchanged knowing glances. Mrs O'Sullivan poked Father Phelan in the ribs with the tip of her elbow. Father Phelan reacted. "Perhaps you would like me to accompany you. There may be some ruffians abroad at this hour of night."

He stared at the priest. "I walked the streets of this town during the civil unrest we experienced some twenty years ago and suffered no injury from anyone of any class or creed or particular station in life, Irishman or Englishman. As for what you call hooligans, they scarcely exist. The only people who caused me any difficulty, though admittedly slight, were your rather ardent friends the republicans. Please go to bed, both of you. I am perfectly able to take care of myself." He stood his ground, and they theirs. Eventually under his obstinate gaze they retreated, each muttering: "Good-night, Canon." He made no effort to reciprocate their civility.

He slipped quietly from the house and briefly considered taking the sacrament but decided against it on the grounds that were he to do so he might well have to forfeit a visit to the girl. Her parents would be present and he longed intensely for the intimacy he had known on his last visit when cradling her in his arms they entered the act of prayer and adoration together. It had been, and still was, a source of great joy to him, though unhappiness had come with the parting. If, as they believed, a visitation was taking place, such intimacy would be impossible. Bran came crashing through from the kitchen just as he was about to leave. He patted the animal's head, spoke softly, then commanded it to stay. With a sharp yelp the dog settled obediently on its haunches.

The waning moon was luminous. Everything cast shadows which were faintly grey rather than deeply black. The gravelled drive crunched noisily beneath his feet. Having gone a few paces he turned and faced the house squarely; he saw the curtains in Father Phelan's room stir and felt the hot rush of anger break on his cheeks when he realised that he was being spied upon. He stared audaciously at the window for some time to allow Father Phelan to know he had been caught like a scullery-maid peeking about on her first day. Turning at the top of the avenue, he was confronted by the many steps which fell in series of sevens to the street far below.

He had a perfect view of the greater part of town. Moonlit it was marvellously still and crisp. The shadows were of varying density. They cut across the moonwhite streets in a combination of angular shapes which bore no relatioin to the rather squat upright buildings which cast them. It was difficult to believe that sleeping in their beds were the people who came to him or his fellow priests for forgiveness of what he considered their minor transgressions. He had not been out at night for many years. With increasing age he left the night-calls to his younger assistants and his parishioners preferred it that way. A fact he somewhat regretted.

He had a fleeting vision of 'Rathbolgan', perfectly silver in moonlight, the vast ancient trees casting deep, calm shadows in the spread of parkland surrounding the house. John took him on occasional expeditions to the weir to see the shining salmon as they threshed furiously in their efforts to gain the upper reaches of the river. Sometimes they walked in silence for mile after mile, their light canvas shoes soaking up the heavy dew, experiencing the fresh night air, the stillness, the pungent scent of grass beneath their feet as they walked. A dog barking sharply in the distance, perhaps, the soft sound of the river as it flowed deeply on. John swam in the broad strip of the river within the estate known as the 'straights'. It was sternly forbidden to them by their grandfather even in the daytime because of its trailing underwater growths, its deep holes and deceptively small whirlpools which had been known to take a few lives in the past. A fine and skilful swimmer, John nevertheless dared the straights. Like the proverbial splendid savage John ran through the wild grasses and reeds on the banks of the river, yelling and roaring in glee. Ironically he drowned not in the dangerous straights but in a stretch of the river further upstream deemed perfectly safe for bathing.

He reached the church gates and taking the cumbersome keys from his pocket selected one and opened the padlock, carefully securing it once he had passed through and drawn the gates shut behind him. He moved quickly down Church Street and turned right into Main Street. Above Deasey's grocery shop a light showed through the curtained window, the faint flicker of a candle. Mr Deasey, a chronic insomniac, was whiling away the long hours of night by reading from his large collection of Zane Grey novels. At Norton's shoeshop someone stepped from the recess between the plate glass windows and planted himself squarely in his path, as if waylaying a thief. He recognised

Sergeant O'Leary who acknowledged him in turn and apologised, saluting smartly. He bade the tall, heavily built man, whose breath smelt of whiskey, a pleasant goodnight and declined his offer of escort the rest of the way.

He remembered how some twenty years or more ago one was liable to be shot on sight if caught abroad at such an hour, even if one had written exemption from the military authorities who had imposed martial law. He had received such licence, the only priest in the entire diocese to do so. It had not endeared him to the town's nationalists who ignored the fact that he risked being shot by drunken Black and Tans, permit or no permit. On such a night as this he had attended a dying woman and having seen her die peacefully had set out to return to the Parochial House, refusing adamantly the company of the husband and son of the dead woman. Both, he realised, would be in far greater danger than he was ever likely to be. A man from Noonan's Court had broken curfew to summon a doctor for his wife in difficult childbirth. He had been wantonly murdered by a drunken soldier who had made no effort to check the man's credentials or the reason why he risked death by breaking the curfew. He had been shot down before O'Brien's newspaper shop. He remembered vividly the blood, which seemed as dark as molten tar in the deceptive moonlight, as it poured from the massive wound in the man's head. It pooled on the foothpath and then trickled down a gentle outward slope to the dusty gutter. Thanks to the intervention of an army officer who chanced by, they had gained entry to O'Brien's shop and thus the man was afforded some semblance of dignity as he died. The spot became a scene of vulgar devotion for some time. Old crones set up an altar with a picture of the Sacred Heart. Those moved by the man's death brought flowers and a tiny flickering flame burned all day and into the early hours of the morning when the old woman who cared for it ceased her vigil. She tired of her devotion and indeed the man's murder was quickly forgotten.

He hurried on wondering why he should be so preoccupied with the death of a man so many years before and whose name now eluded him. He hurried across the bridge, the wide span of the river now shallow in high summer and smelling sweetly, sickeningly of sewage and other waste. He turned down Mill Street. A light shone in the O'Dowd House. He thought Mrs O'Dowd might in fact be with the Maddens and felt a brief surge of resentment.

His footsteps rang loudly and clearly in the deserted street. Sound, he noted, seemed to soar and curl about the chimney pots of the silent, moonlit buildings. He turned down Copley's Lane.

He was admitted to the Madden household. Two lighted candles burned on the kitchen table flanking an upright crucifix. Both man and wife were huddled about the lighted range as though perished with the cold. They were plainly glad to see him and their eyes, as they turned to him, held a strong appeal. Light flooded down the steep staircase as if from an immensely powerful source.

He indicated quietly that he wished to go upstairs alone. He mounted the stairs carefully and entered the girl's bedroom. She was in her bed, her black hair loose and lovely on either side of her head. Her face was radiant and from her eyes shone the bright light of unconcealable love. She was beautiful. More beautiful than any living being he had ever seen. She seemed revivified in every way, the ravages of her fatal disease set at naught. Her eyes were focussed on the end of the bed and her lips moved in silent conversation.

He tried to bring himself to turn towards the source of the brilliant and mysterious light. He could not move his body towards the left, some force was impeding all movement in that direction. Before he quite realised what he was doing, he was on his knees, his head bowed and deep in silent worship. He knelt totally engrossed in his prayer and possessed by love and peace. He remained so until the faint light of dawn began to assert itself. The intense light gradually dimmed. He experienced sorrow. The girl suffered too, but far greater than he. He saw as much by her eyes. She smiled sadly the smile peculiar to lovers on parting and then drifted into deep, obliterative sleep. He remained on his knees totally undone by what he had seen and experienced and grieved at his humanity, the essential clay that is ordained man's state.

Rising he kissed the sleeping figure on the brow, taking his leave of her. Downstairs they both glanced at him anxiously, the strain of the events of the last few days showing clearly. He considered what he might say to them. They were expecting some comfort in their unease and some assurance that whatever the cause or source of the phenomenon he himself had just witnessed, it was not intrinsically evil. He nevertheless felt that he could not deem it the work of God as they might understand the use of the term. He himself did not believe in the existence of a deity; how then could he proclaim the visitations which so perplexed them as the work of God? He could not account to anyone for what he had seen in rational terms. It lay very definitely in the realm of the supernatural though not possibly within the meaning of that word as he himself would have understood it in the days of his firmest belief. He considered the two most striking factors of his experience of the event. It's great beauty, the great goodness which radiated from the unseen source of light and which had permeated not only the entire room but, or so it seemed, every fibre of his being as it had undoubtedly enraptured the body and soul of the dying girl.

He turned towards them and spoke deliberately. "I believe we are in the presence of what I can only regard as grace," he found himself saying, "possibly the very presence of God. I believe your daughter is being singularly honoured and blessed and that there is therefore nothing to fear." Pleasure and relief alike showed instantly on their faces. They exchanged glances. "Nevertheless," he continued sternly, "I must again caution you and pledge you to strict silence. I beg you to ask your neighbours who might be aware of what is happening to guard their tongues and not speculate too much on the origins or meanings of these extraordinary events. I ask you to pray, earnestly and at all times. I shall do likewise." The woman wept shortly but not sorrowfully, the husband seemed incapable of looking directly at him as if to keep hidden the depth of his emotions. He declined gracefully to take some tea as he had to keep his fast until he had said his daily mass. They understood and to expressions of their deepest gratitude he took his leave.

He ignored those still clustered about the doorways and made his way back to the Parochial House. The streets were brightening and at Patrick's Lane he saw a shadow scurry furtively up the hill and turn into the Back Quays. It was he knew without doubt Father Phelan who had obviously followed him to keep watch. That he had been followed and spied upon did not disturb him. The man's motives, he thought absently, were of the highest. He resisted the temptation to dwell too much upon what he had experienced. He did not think of it as divine yet he did not despair. He was prepared to have things reveal themselves as they might.

Later he said his mass and found his sense of service to others renewed. He passed the day in a state of elation which he knew to be hazardous but he could do nothing to relieve it. Later in the afternoon he went to the poplars walk at the top of the cemetery so frequented by Father Good in his more romantic moods. He tried but failed to pray. Twice Father Phelan called him for his evening meal. Twice he reassured the priest he would join them shortly. Finally Mrs O'Sullivan herself appeared and delivered what amounted to an ultimatum. He told her to serve the others.

He would if necessary have his food cold. Muttering rebelliously, she returned to the house. His mood gradually became more tranquil. He continued to stroll the path until dusk began to gather. He felt content and yet expectant of great things to come.

7

He awoke in the early hours of the morning. The room was partially in gloom. The light lacked the sharp definity of the sunny mornings which they had enjoyed since the good spell of weather began some weeks before. He thought upon waking that he had heard a cry of distress, low and chilling. He listened intently: he could hear nothing but the abiding silence of the house and the sleeping town. A goods train shunted slowly and approached. Its sharp piercing whistle sounded with shattering effect as it approached the tunnel directly under the flight of steps from the church to the street below.

He recalled lying awake during the early hours of the morning in his childhood, ears pricked as the sleeping city stirred and began to function like some big, benign animal awaking from its slumber. Dray horses, iron-shod and their cart wheels hooped in steel bands, beginning their day of relentless labour. Horses in many instances better sheltered and fed than the poor or even those whose task was to work with them all day. He had soon learned to distinguish the various monasteries, convents and the houses of religious orders by their distinctive bells which not always simultaneously struck the morning angelus and, blessing himself, he would whisper the prayers commemorating the annunciation, his first act of devotion of the day. He felt the pressures of the past assert themselves and angered he leaned aside and switched on the bedside lamp. He selected a crime novel and tried to read it but his eyes remained steadfastly focussed on the first few words and refused to scan further.

She was suffering, he knew. For some days past she was in extremity and the end could be expected now at any moment. He found himself beseeching the powers of heaven that she might die cleanly and well, as only one who had suffered so immeasurably deserved. All traces of the beauty illness had infused her with had now vanished. She now had the features of a harrowed old woman and she was wretchedly reduced in stature and weight. He hoped that he might be permitted one last grace, that of attending her in her last earthly moments, that he might speed her onwards to whatever lay ahead with extreme unction. Prayers he thought brave and heroic and worthy of the great fortitude the fragile faithful usually summoned as they departed this world. It was his earnest hope, his greatest expectation, that she might bequeath to him in her dying moments her imperishable faith. He thought it his only hope and dreaded that she might die and he would not be by her side.

When last he had taken the sacrament to her she had, while in his embrace, replied with astonishing clarity of speech and mind to a question he had put to her on impulse, believing she would be incapable of reply. "What is your expectation my child?" And she replied with a strenuous effort to speak clearly, "The hope of heaven, the presence of God." For some seconds she seemed possessed of a great strength of body, mind and purpose, then she had lapsed into a semi-coma. Her remark had overawed him. He treasured it as the testimony of one of great spirit and he became convinced that somehow, somewhere, some part of man despite his adamite inheritance, was indestructible, and she, the love of his life, would attain glory.

He felt a sharp stab across his chest. He knew the pain was not physical. He cried out in terror at the anguish which appeared to threaten his life. With a broad sweeping movement he swept aside all the articles which cluttered his bedside table. They crashed noisily onto the floor. He screamed out like an animal fatally wounded not by one clean blow but by a multitude of lesser ones which pained individually to some extent, but accumulatively agonised most massively. He heard the light being switched on in Father Phelan's room. Shortly after he sensed someone at his door. He tried, but failed to cry out. She had died he knew, quietly and in her sleep.

Father Phelan helped him back onto his bed. He again tried to speak but could only mutter incoherently. The curate spoke reassuringly. "It's alright, Canon. Nothing to worry about. A spasm of some kind." He took the pulse of his superior now shivering violently. It was rapid but not critically so, nevertheless he felt he could not accept responsibility. Summoning Mrs O'Sullivan from her room he told her to dress and come to the Canon. He would in the meanwhile call Doctor Barrett.

It was some time before he succeeded in arousing anyone in the doctor's house. Doctor Barrett answered himself and assured him he would be over as soon as possible. Father Phelan entered the kitchen and riddling the slumbering banked fire, fed it some tinder and hard, well dried peat. He put on a kettle and returned to the Canon's room. He asked Mrs O'Sullivan to make some tea.

Phelan looked at the man in the bed with curious detachment. He was still in a state of shock but had lapsed into silence. He was salivating heavily and it dribbled from the corner of his mouth. He made no effort to assist him in any way or make him more comfortable. He knew he would receive little thanks and besides there remained a residual hatred of his superior from the days when he used to drink too much and the Canon had condemned him. Now he felt free to subject the man to some, though passive, abuse. It gave him he realised, a very definite pleasure. He took a packet of cigarettes from the pocket of his dressing gown and, opening a window wide to avoid filling the room with smoke, he lit one and smoked absently while awaiting the arrival of Doctor Barrett.

The girl, Phelan guessed, had died and inexplicably but yet understandably the Canon had realised as much. He had seen the bond which sometimes grew between patient and physician, between priest and dying. To a degree, in some unexplainable manner they became an extension of one's self. If not in attendance at the bedside one frequently sensed their moment of death, possibly in the same way primitive communities became aware almost collectively of the death of one in their midst. It was an aspect of the priesthood he found disturbing and rarely if ever pondered.

The telephone jolted the curate. It rang persistently and eventually he heard Mrs O'Sullivan, who had some fear of it, answer. Father Good, he realised with no surprise, had not put in an appearance. He had the cunning of the weak and faced problems only when inescapably confronted with them. The housekeeper entered the room. Miss Madden, she whispered, had died in her sleep some time ago. They had been unable to summon the Canon as he had wished them to, because the death, though expected, had come suddenly. He could well imagine with what stunning force it had in fact come.

"Who," Phelan asked, "made the telephone call?" Mrs O'Dowd had, she informed him. Shortly she retreated to the kitchen and returned with a mug of tea and in her confusion offered it to him. The curate shook his head and indicated the Canon. He himself had to maintain his fast to say mass later in the morning. But the temptation to drink the sweet smelling brew was very strong. He tried to cool some tea on the spoon before offering it to the Canon but he could not swallow and once nearly choked on what little passed his lips.

Father Phelan gave the tea back to Mrs O'Sullivan and asked

her to call Father Good. The Maddens would be distressed and one of the priests of the parish should visit to pray for the deceased and offer condolences. Father Good could do so before going to the convent to say the early morning mass for the nuns.

The physician arrived shortly after. He consulted with Father Phelan who then withdrew, leaving him alone with the Canon. "Good morning, Canon. I believe you had bad news. The Madden girl, young Catherine. If it's any comfort to you she was in a coma for the better part of three days and therefore suffered no pain. No pain whatever. She died gently, for which we may well both thank God."

He felt the doctor's thumb and finger on his wrist. The Canon tried to speak but succeeded in grunting. The doctor continued, his voice soft, considerate, remote. "You cannot say I failed in my duty by not warning you. I warned you very firmly and explicitly. I made my position very clear indeed. Now you are in extreme shock. I now have to take certain measures to protect your health, loathe though I am to do so. Do I have your permission to take these steps?"

The patient clenched his hands tightly. He sensed what they would entail. He spoke only with great difficulty. "I have a duty to perform. A binding duty."

"So have I, Canon. And I intend carrying out my obligations. I want you to enter a nursing home at Harbour View. You will quite like it there. It is of course by the sea, a simply splendid bay, and nearby parkland area with fine sheltered walks. You will be pleased to know it is not run by an order of nuns but by a Nurse Beamish, a personal friend of mine. What do you say to that?"

"I have a duty to perform . . ."

"You do not like it. I thought not. Nevertheless I must insist this time, Canon. I must insist."

"I have a duty. . . . One last duty to perform."

Doctor Barrett smiled. He spoke good humouredly as he would to the spoilt child of one of his wealthier patients. "What you feel obliged to do can easily be done by Father Phelan or Father Good. The girl is beyond all mortal help. As for spiritual help, well, you can pray here as well as in the girl's home."

"I wish to see her. I must see her." His words were slurred like those of someone afflicted with a speech impediment.

Doctor Barrett shook his head. "No. It is quite out of the question. I absolutely forbid it."

He rounded in fury on the doctor. "You are in no position to forbid me anything in accordance with my priestly duties. That prerogative is strictly reserved to my Lord Bishop. Do you understand that, Doctor?" He paused, unaware that in his fury he had fully regained his power of speech.

Doctor Barrett fell silent. He gazed at the dull cream wallpaper on the wall directly opposite as though it merited close and careful scrutiny. He took his bag which he had brought with him, extended a hand in farewell which was ignored and murmuring rather sharply, "Good morning, Canon," he left the room.

He sat on the bed exhausted by the scene. His last speech to the doctor had drained every reserve. He pressed the buzzer attached to the wall above the bedside table. Mrs O'Sullivan responded, concerned and rather edgy. "Please instruct Father Phelan to announce that there will be no early mass this morning due to unforeseen events. Please see that under no circumstances am I disturbed by anyone. Draw the blinds and curtains before you leave." She crossed to the windows to comply with his last command. As soon as she had left the room he turned his face to the wall and numb with grief, dozed, worn out as if after a long testing battle. Once or twice he stirred to a physical aching which almost prevented him from breathing. He had forgotten the savagery of death, its air of filthy pillage, its mean stealth. He wept once, shortly and briefly and mercifully slumbered again. The strain of the last few months had taken their toll. He slept deeply though subject to black dreams. Once or twice he called her by name. Catherine. Father Phelan roused him gently.

He noticed the man then glared at him in anger. Father Phelan appeared quite unperturbed by his display. "Miss Madden's remains are to be removed to the church this evening, Canon. I thought it best to wake you for some breakfast. Then you can rest until you go to the funeral, as I have no doubt you wish to do." He hesitated. "You slept all day and night, Canon, and as I am now responsible for your welfare during your indisposition I took the liberty of asking Doctor O'Malley to see if he approves of the arrangement." Father Phelan lapsed into silence. He had spoken most respectfully but his voice had a cold edge to it and in his eyes battle gleamed. The Canon was quiet for some seconds and tried to think clearly. Father Phelan, he knew, had the advantage and could prevent him from attending the funeral if he wished. "That was very prudent of you, Father Phelan. Where is Doctor O'Malley?"

"He is outside, Canon."

"Please raise the blinds and draw the curtains and then show him in."

Doctor O'Malley entered. As always he was dressed rather untidily in good but badly-cared-for clothes. He sported grey tweeds, stout brown shoes and a Trinity College tie. A young man of lean, angular build, he had narrow, close-set eyes which were so deeply brown they might be described as black. He had a sallow complexion and black curly hair, close cut, already receding. Altogether he had the look of the brooding, savage Celt. A solitary man, he was subject to bouts of depression during which he withdrew from social contact and kept to his room in the Munster Arms Hotel. Inexplicably for such a humane man, he liked the shoot and would gleefully participate in the slaughter of any amount of game irrespective of the kind. Some wildfowl or rabbits he distributed to friends of his but he killed numbers far in excess of even the generous limits of good sportsmanship. Relations between them were not amicable. Doctor O'Malley had some years ago attended a woman in the now demolished area known as Irishtown, a poor neighbourhood which had existed since shortly after the famine of eighteen-forty-seven when the dispossessed natives had been allowed to settle because they could be a supply of cheap labour for the town's few industrial factories rather than for any humanitarian reasons. The woman in question, a Mrs Lawlor, was in bad health. Married of necessity when she was sixteen, she had by the age of twenty-five some eight children and was in appearance an old, haggard woman, worn down by toil and worry and the demands made on her by such a large family. Her husband was an unlettered labourer. He drank, but not excessively and was not by nature mean or ill-disposed towards his wife. He was simply uncouth, incapable of controlling his sexual appetite which was considerable. Hardly had his wife given birth to one child than she again conceived, to the detriment of her health. Finally Doctor O'Malley was convinced that future childbearing would place the woman's life in jeopardy. On medical grounds he advised her to have an operation which would preclude further pregnancy. The woman had sought the advice of the Canon. After discussing the matter fully with a prominent catholic gynaecologist in the city who had in turn examined the woman and failed to reach the same conclusion as Doctor O'Malley, the woman was pronounced healthy and capable of childbearing. In due course she did conceive and died at the birth. Her husband took to drinking heavily and was found dead on the railway lines some distance from his house. There was little doubt that it had been suicide and that the man was in a disturbed state and he had therefore been accorded a Christian burial. His family had been dispersed amongst several religious foundations in the city and county. In an alcoholic frenzy Doctor O'Malley had confronted him publicly and had slandered him and abused him in the foulest manner possible. He had on legal advice not proceeded against the man in a court of law but had lodged a formal complaint against the doctor with the County Medical Board. The doctor had been severely reprimanded by the authorities. Nevertheless he still retained the loyalties of his patients and he, the Canon, could be said to have come out of the matter less favourably.

Doctor O'Malley pretended no great warmth or affection. "How are you, Canon Fitzgerald?"

His reply was equally frigid. "Quite well, thank you."

"Father Phelan has asked me to give you a thorough examination, merely as a precaution. May I do so?"

Father Phelan, distinctly unhappy, gazed sightlessly before him.

"Please do, Doctor O'Malley. One must take extra care in a case such as this."

The curate and the doctor exchanged glances. Father Phelan, now more miserable than ever, resumed his gazing into vacancy. Doctor O'Malley began his examination. The curate, muttering an excuse, attempted to leave the room. The doctor then said, "Please remain until the examination is complete, Father Phelan."

The curate coloured and directed his gaze to the polished linoleum on the floor. The Canon frowned for the insult, he knew, was calculated. He resisted with some effort the temptation to pass a bitter comment because he thought it wiser to hold his tongue; this man could prevent him from attending to his important duty, the short ceremonies which conclude a Christian life.

Doctor O'Malley finished his examination and deliberated for some seconds. Then he gave his considered judgement. "You are suffering from exhaustion and nervous stress. It would be wise to take a rest for a few weeks. A month or two perhaps. There are plenty of nursing homes I can recommend. If you do not agree now you will be forced to do so in the very near future, and probably will be incapacitated for a longer period. Possibly, just possibly, it might then be a question of a suitable hospital rather than a nursing home." He drew breath. "However, I gather from Father Phelan that you are reluctant to follow the advice of my colleague Dr Barrett on the matter. I can hardly expect you to follow mine." He paused and then spoke with icy clarity. "I will allow you two days to make arrangements to enter a nursing home or I myself will see they are made and you will have to submit. Otherwise, I too will refuse all responsibility for you."

The silence was leaden. Doctor O'Malley placed his stethoscope in his bag. Father Phelan appeared uncertain what to do or say or even where to look; sweat gathered on his forehead and trickled down his face; for some reason or other he did not use his handkerchief.

"I take it it is your intention to walk in this funeral, Canon?" It was the custom of the parish that the priests officiating at the funeral would precede the cortege wearing broad white sashes over their greatcoats. "Yes," he replied briefly, "I am, as is the custom." Doctor O'Malley nodded his head shortly. "It would be wisest not to walk, but on the other hand, if you collapse there will be plenty there to come to your assistance and resuscitate you if necessary." On that note of frankness he left the room without farewell and curtly indicated to Father Phelan that he needed no escort to the front door.

He refused to meet Father Phelan's eyes. "Please ask Mrs O'Sullivan to bring me some hot water to wash and shave and ask her also to lay out suitable clothes." He lapsed into sullen silence. Feeling himself dismissed, Father Phelan left the room. He lay still, smarting from Doctor O'Malley's insolent behaviour but somehow grateful that he had not forced him to stay away from the funeral. He felt that despite the antipathy which existed between them Doctor O'Malley was not altogether without sympathy. After some time he pulled back the bedclothes with considerable difficulty and by retracting his legs and thighs managed to swing over the side of the bed. He felt wretchedly weak. Darkness swarmed like an enemy about his head which seemed to swim, but he held tight and the giddiness receded. Clutching nearby furniture he managed to make his way to the armchair by the fireside. He sat there miserably, a frail, spent figure in a nightshirt which gave him little dignity.

Catherine had in the very end eluded him and brought all his vague and insubstantial hopes to nothing. She had carried away her great legacy of sanctity and goodness without affording him access to the mysterious source of her blessedness. She had failed to bequeath to him the fragile fruit of her suffering. He experienced emotional bareness such as he had not felt since the death of his mother, the last immediate member of his family.

Father Good entered with a large jug of hot water and managed, with some agility, to carry a small shaving mug of steaming water and, draped across his right arm, two clean towels. He laid everything on the wash-stand with ritualistic correctness and murmured apologetically, "Mrs O'Sullivan asked me to bring these up, Canon. She's not feeling well." He guessed the young priest was lying. His housekeeper, whom he had known the greater part of his life — though not intimately — and the junior priest of his parish feared him with the terrible fear the Irish reserve for those they believe to be unbalanced or altogether mad. Father Good exuded cowardice despite his best efforts. "Thank you, Father. That was kind of you. Tell Mrs O'Sullivan I hope she soon recovers from what is, I hope, a minor indisposition."

He bowed his head and found himself wishing that he could slip into perpetual sleep and know no further torment. He rallied, assuring himself that in twenty-four hours it would all be over. She, Catherine, would be laid in the earth with all the others, the departed and he would have to control himself. He could only hope that in the few years left to him before he too died, he might draw strength from the memories of her. She was above all else, true and valiant and would not desert him. Then he too would lie with the dead, be ceremoniously if shortly mourned and in time be forgotten. Man's destiny is no greater than that of a leaf. It buds and grows, then fades and falls to the earth beneath and is soon rendered dust.

He roused himself reluctantly, rose and made his way to the wash-stand. He thought of requesting Father Phelan's assistance but refused to submit himself further to physical dependence on one he had come to heartily if irrationally to hate. Draping the towel about his waist, he began the arduous task of shaving himself whilst trying to remain upright. Outside the air was sharp and crystal. An evening of close perspective which augured rain. Distantly a goods train shunted slowly. Some children at play shrieked and a dog yelped disconsolately. The journey on foot to the Madden house would not, he thought, be excessively tiring, in what he imagined would be a cool evening. He would not hasten, allowing himself ample time to reach the house at the appointed time. And he noted somewhat grimly, there was more than a grain of truth in what Doctor O'Malley had said about collapsing. Savagely put, he thought, remembering the words. But admirably succinct. He gathered strength moment by moment and he found that having shaved he could wash his body more easily. Donning his night shirt and dressing gown, he put on his slippers and pressed the buzzer by his bedside table to summon his housekeeper. Once, he thought, to summon Mrs O'Sullivan, twice for Father Phelan and three times in the unlikely event of ever wishing to call Father Good.

She responded surprisingly quickly considering her illness of less than ten minutes ago. Clearly she had been weeping. Her face was swollen and flushed and rather ugly. There was some fear, subdued but nevertheless present, as she enquired politely, "Yes, Canon?"

"My suit, Mrs O'Sullivan, and something to eat, something light. Toast perhaps and some tea." "I have the dinner kept for you below. Maybe you'd like to have a bit. You haven't eaten properly for days." He shook his head. "I think not, thank you. Something light." Nodding her head in compliance, she left him.

He sought his breviary and saw to his annoyance it was not in its proper place. He found it eventually and turned to the office of the day. His marker indicated that it was Sunday, which was clearly wrong. He tried to remember the day of the week and found himself too exhausted to do so with any clarity. He tried to place the events of the last few days in proper sequence but found he could not. There was no calendar in the room and no newspaper to help him determine the day. Mrs O'Sullivan, he remembered irritably, kept them to read in bed, which she did with obsessive thoroughness, extracting obscure details she found fascinating and loved to discuss with Father Phelan and Father Good in particular. He flicked the breviary open deciding that the office of any day taken at random would have to suffice. The intention rather than the deed was more important he assured himself. He attempted to read but found the effort too much and so he laid it aside.

He was staring idly at last winter's disintegrating ferns when his housekeeper brought him light supper on a tray. "A bowl of porridge, Canon. Take some. It will help keep your strength up." He nodded non-committedly. For no good reason he was tempted to ask her where Bran was. Out with Father Phelan he thought somewhat enviously; he had not heard his distinctive bark all afternoon. He refrained from making any enquiry.

The whining of a dog aroused him. He found to his dismay that he had been in a trance-like state. He certainly had not been asleep. He had no memory of having eaten or drunk, yet the tray was bare of food, the teapot empty. He heard the evening angelus bell and sat as if transmuted into stone. He had been, he realised, hoping that this hour would never strike. That somehow it would be withheld and he would not have to perform the last ceremonies which would mark her descent into the earth, her entry into death's vast domain. He drew a long deep breath and went downstairs.

Mrs O'Sullivan handed him his wide-brimmed hat but he took his biretta instead. She gave him his ceremonial breviary and shook out his white sash which she then draped across his shoulder. Father Phelan and Father Good both stood waiting in the hallway, suitably dressed and sashed. They seemed anxious to attend to his needs. Bran came through from the kitchen licking his wet chops, obviously having just drank some water. He barked delightedly and curled about his legs playfully. Suddenly the Canon gave vent to his rage. He roughly shoved the dog from him and then kicked him with his booted foot. The dog yelped in pain and betrayal and slunk down the hall, his tail between his legs. No sooner had he struck than he realised how venomous and mean an act it was. He felt that he would weep and to avoid doing so he addressed Mrs O'Sullivan roughly. "Please keep that animal under some control, Mrs O'Sullivan."

She glanced at him, anger burning in her eyes. "Yes, Canon," she replied in what was unmistakably fury as she held the door open for him. He passed through, pausing on the lower step of the short flight. He heard the door close behind the two priests who had followed him out. It was closed less than gently and after a second or so he could hear Mrs O'Sullivan speak comfortingly to the dog.

He walked onto the gravelled drive in silence and unbidden his priests followed some two steps behind him. He made no effort to make conversation, nor did they. They made their way down the flights of steps to Church Street and continued along Main Street. As he had thought, it was indeed an evening of near perspective. The design and for the most part the harmony of the buildings, particularly the older ones in the square, were sharply defined in the heightened evening light and he saw as though for the first time. The Bank of Ireland — a handsome neo-classic building — and the stark linear beauty of the Courthouse — emphasised by its partial cover of virginia creeper, its leaves now limp after the day's heat — commanded the respect due to them. He found his senses in general heightened by the tension, especially his sight and hearing. Long before they reached the bridge he heard the musical sound of the shallow waters. There might be, he thought, a salmon lying in one of the deeper pools, in which case one of the fair-headed Lees might be trying to catch him.

The draught from the river struck him as they approached. A startlingly nauseating stench of stagnant water, trapped sewage and the effluence from the town's butchers shops, whose staff slaughtered their cattle in filthy conditions. It almost overwhelmed him. He staggered. His biretta fell from his head and rolled into the gutter choked with litter and a mixture of dust and phlegm recently discharged from the throats of passers-by. He felt his entrails contract. He grasped frantically for air. Father

Phelan grasped him about the waist before he fell and propped him against the wall. He heard his assistant murmur: "You had better take some of this, Canon," and before he realised what was happening, still less protest, the priest had thrust the mouth of a hip-flask between his teeth; tilting it, he had poured some whiskey on his tongue and then angled his head in such a way that he had no alternative but to swallow. The scalding liquid stung his mouth and burned his throat. He felt his stomach heave as the whiskey entered it. Nausea again began to rise. "You had better have some more, Canon," Father Phelan said dryly and not without malice, adding under his breath, "Easy to see you're not used to it." Before he could take any action the process was repeated. "There!" said the curate with relish. "If you vomit you have something to bring up."

He leaned on the parapet of the bridge. A swastika had been painstakingly cut into the solid granite of the central commemorative stone, its surface worn smooth by the corner-boys who gathered there to sit in the fine summers' evenings. It was a recent addition to the usual raw obscenities which however were merely scratched upon the surface. He gazed downriver to where the river rounded a bend and was lost to sight. Down there were the shallows by Copley's Lane and close by, the house of the dead girl, their immediate destination. His head began to clear. His stomach warmed. All traces and feelings of nausea passed away. He found he could take huge gulps of the foul air and not feel sickened. A slight, stale breeze was blowing upriver and ruffled his sparse hair. The waters sparkled and the sky was washed with saffron as the sun, which was directly behind him, began its slow descent to the horizon.

Father Good was assiduously dusting his biretta with his handkerchief. Father Phelan relinquished his hold on him. "Are you alright now, Canon?"

"Thank you, " he replied shortly, "I feel much better. Could I please have my biretta?" Father Good handed it to him solemnly as though it represented ultimate authority. He took it and planted it on his head without ceremony. After taking a few hesitant steps he discovered he was quite in control and strode forward boldly.

Reaching Mill Street he saw that the first houses had their blinds drawn, Mrs O'Dowd's amongst them. Further down in less prosperous cottages he found that the blinds had been drawn in some and pictures of a religious nature draped in mourning crepe had been hung from the window catches. Others, their blinds undrawn, displayed pictures flanked with unlit candles wedged in the unlikeliest of holders. A few had only an unlit candle in the window. He stared silently in distaste at what he considered an excess of cheap emotion. She was deserving of more than this tawdry recognition. Dignified and sombre facades would have been more becoming.

The street was thronged. As far as the eye could see people were milling about in their Sunday-best clothes. Women predominated but nevertheless the number of men present was considerable. To his chagrin they had to leave the foothpath and take to the road. As if before a swinging scythe, a swarth opened ahead of them as the crowd parted to allow them to progress.

At the corner of Copley's Lane they found themselves facing a solid mass of impacted humanity all seeking to press down the lane towards the Madden house. Here in the laneway itself every house had its windows stripped of blinds and curtains and in them stood blazing candles, mute witness to depth of feelings aroused by the death of the girl. Despite himself he was impressed that so simple a young woman could evoke so deep a response. Tears welled in his eyes and he coughed fastidiously to prevent himself uttering a sob. Father Phelan wormed his way from behind and roughly cut a pathway through the throng, allowing them to move forward. His old horrors of being touched asserted themselves and he felt sickened and repelled by the swirling crowd about him. He was sweating freely and again felt weak and feared he might not be capable of withstanding the strain of what yet lay ahead. Word of their approach, instead of compelling people to part and make way as they would respectfully do under more normal circumstances, gave rise to a low cry of dismay with unmistakably ugly undertones and the mass became a mob and surged forward with added desperation and determination. He knew they had not seen the girl in death and were determined to do so, though whether from respect for the deceased or the baser motive of curiosity, he dared not speculate.

As they reached the house they heard the wail of keening women, some of whom he knew by sight. Dirty, unkempt wretches, they hovered about the houses of the dead and keened a chant which was hideously primitive, the sole remnant of their native pagan culture. It never failed to chill his blood and engender if not hatred, outright but subdued rage. The hair at the nape of his neck bristled. He set his jaw knowing he would have to drive the harpies from the house before he could even think of commencing the funeral prayers. Their drunken voices defiled the occasion and traduced the memory of the brave and faithful Catherine. Cold seething anger churned inside him. He forced his way forward with a churlish lack of civility.

Mrs Madden, all in newly-bought black, sat on a kitchen chair, her short and stubby form looking as if it had been unseemly wedged into its position with some effort. She wore a black grosgrain costume. Her swollen feet were forced tightly into new black shoes and altogether she appeared slightly grotesque. In a chair by her sat her husband, dressed in deep blue serge and wearing a black tie and crepe armband about the sleeve of his right arm. His nose was continuously dripping droplets of water which he kept wiping away with a handkerchief. Other than a certain bright light in his eyes, he displayed no signs of grief. They both rose as he entered, taking off his biretta as he did so. He laid it aside on the table and though disliking the idea of physical contact he extended his hand to take theirs and offer his commiserations, inclining forward in what was meant to be a courtly, low bow but which he felt must have struck the onlookers as the jerky movement of a marionette. He also shook hands with two plump women whose hands were loathsomely warm and fleshy. Dressed in black, they were unmistakably Mrs Madden's sisters. Like hers, their faces were bloated and red from weeping. Behind him he heard the two priests offering their condolences, Father Good's voice trembling perilously. There was no sign of the girl's four brothers.

One of Mrs Madden's sisters excused herself and scurried upstairs; she could be heard urging those in the deathroom to leave as the priests had arrived to conduct the last prayers for Catherine in what had been her home. They seemed reluctant to acquiesce and eventually the keeners moved only after loud protest. One sharp featured woman in a dark shawl came downstairs with a scowl on her face as heavy as a thundercloud and clutching to her bosom a very large, framed picture of Our Lady of Perpetual Succour.

He realised that the people had been bringing religious objects with which to touch the body of the dead girl whom in their own way they thought of as being sanctified. It displeased him to witness such witless devotion. He stared at them in stark contempt. They for their part resented his intrusion and were loath to leave the house.

A woman whom he recognised but did not know, came downstairs. Shabbily dressed, she was bandy legged and carried a cheap shopping bag made of sacking. She wore a pale blue coat. Her stockings were ripped in places and her shoes cracked and broken. She was known to be mentally unstable and, though gentle by nature, given to wild bouts of irrational rage. Her hair was greasy and stuck together in ragged plaits. In all probability it was lice-infested. She approached Mrs Madden and grasping her by the hand told her aloud that instead of weeping it was down on her knees she should be, thanking God for having a daughter a saint in heaven and not a streel or a dirty stop-out who would disgrace them for all time by getting into trouble with some man. She scratched her head vigorously and, her mouth flecked with spittle, she turned to him for confirmation. "Isn't that so, Canon?" He refrained from comment.

He glanced at the mirror on the wall to the right of the doorway and noted that strangely it had not been covered with a linen cloth as was the custom. It was a small mirror he decided and had therefore been overlooked.

The woman chattering to Mrs Madden became increasingly hysterical and seemed determined to remain. Her body odours were now becoming apparent. They were vile. Those of a woman who paid little or no attention to her personal hygiene. Sexual secretions mingled with sour sweat and a cheap and acrid perfume used liberally to scent the unscentable. Mr Madden finally took courage. "I'll see you out, Mrs O'Boyce." Taking the woman tightly by the arm he led her gently but firmly to the doorway, thanking her sincerely for her sympathy and the mass card she had brought with her. Once she was outside the front door was closed. Those still excluded moaned in unison like blooded dogs deprived of sport.

He took his stole from his pocket and draped it about his neck. Father Phelan and Father Good did likewise. Then all mounted the staircase, Father Good as tense as a thoroughbred hunter ready to take flight at the first discordant sound.

He had forgotten that she had been a Child of Mary and was therefore privileged to wear a habit of light blue and a white veil rather than the more common shroud habit of dark brown. On her breast rested the large medallion which signified her membership of the religious society. In death her body had shrunk to a considerable degree. Her face was pinched and drawn, her cheek bones sharply defined as they had never been in life. Far from being a picture of saintly tranquility and indeed beauty, as he had so ardently hoped she would be, her appearance struck him as being bitter. It seemed to nullify all the blessedness he had seen for himself in her eyes and on her lips and which had radiated from her entire being. The sight of her pierced him with pain. He longed inexpressibly to kiss her entwined hands or her brow in final homage but realised the folly of even attempting to do so. He felt as if the veil of the temple was rent and he the sole witness. Taking a sprig of palm from the bedside table he immersed it in a bowl of holy-water and uttering the benediction almost silently he sprinkled the body. He blessed himself, intoning the words loudly and firmly, and kneeling began the few short prayers which in English lacked beauty but in Latin were resonant and majestic. They were soon finished. He looked at the body on the bed, the face locked in the tight cold grip of death and made more pallid by the flickering light of nearby candles. He hesitated, knowing that at this point he should rise and impart absolution. He could not. He bit his lips and tried to subdue a rising tide of emotion which seemed about to unman him. He bowed his head and on impulse struck his breast three times, intoning aloud the great cry of pain which had been wrung from the mouth of the stricken psalmist: "Out of the depths I cry to thee, O Lord! Lord, hear my voice! Let thy ears be attentive to the voice of my supplications! If thou, O Lord, should mark iniquities, Lord, who could stand?" Dimly he realised that both Father Phelan and Father Good had taken up the chant. The words cleft the warm air of the room as one might imagine arrows shot cleanly from a well-tensed bow would do. In the room below and in the laneway outside those who had come to mourn knew there had been a departure from the prescribed procedure. The grief underlying his voice was unmistakable. A ripple of shocked reaction ran through the crowd. The Latin chant came to an end: "Eternal rest grant to her, O Lord. And let perpetual light shine upon her. May she rest in peace. Amen." The chant died on the still, charged air. He heard in the following silence the ripple of water as it ran over the shallows of the river at the end of the lane and realised how very much he had come to love her, suddenly aware of an inner void which would never be filled. It would always be there. Dull, aching, and he, ever exiled.

With an effort he recollected himself and rising he imparted his blessing bringing the service to an end. He lingered, briefly gazing at her face, seeking to impress the memory upon his mind. Poor child, he thought, she has suffered so much. And to what end, he reflected bitterly. There would be no second spring, no new Jerusalem. He turned abruptly and left. The coffin which was to receive her body stood on a trestle in the kitchen. He calculated they would have a considerable problem getting it up the narrow staircase much less down. He watched with an almost brutal detachment when it was manhandled upstairs with the great difficulty he had anticipated. Mrs Madden cried out: "Ah no! No! Oh God NO!" as if the reality of her daughter's death had only now struck her. She tried to clutch the coffin and prevent it from being carried up. Her sisters tried to restrain her. She broke from their grasp and only Mr Madden succeeded by force in holding her; gently he stroked her head and repeated her name in both entreaty and endearment. "Nora, Nora, Nora." The men managed finally to get the coffin upstairs. There was a pause while they transferred the remains from the bed to the coffin. The senior member of the party, a short, stubby man in blue serge and a bowler hat perched on a head of grey curly hair, who exuded self-confidence like some self-satisfied but corrupt politician, asked deferentially: "Would yeself like to come up now, Mam?" As if sleepwalking Mrs Madden moved forward of her own accord, followed by her husband and sisters. Her cries upon reaching the room rent the air. Those of her sisters arose with them. The sounds were heard outside, the keeners who had been virtually driven from the house upon his arrival took up the cry. The evening air was made alive by their wailing. Rigid with displeasure he gripped his breviary wondering how long the unseemly proceedings would last. Finally his patience snapped, he nodded curtly to Father Phelan who opened the door for him; he stepped outside, the others following. The door closed behind them.

The crowd fell silent. Someone tried to sing 'Faith of Our Fathers' in a thin wavering voice. His flesh crawled as if his entire body was suddenly liced. The whole funeral, he feared, was about to descend into low farce, the crowd he sensed, were volatile. Moved consciously by the deepest and sincerest motives, subconsciously they were driven by primitive forces, tribal in origin and nature. This for them was a leavetaking. To thwart them, however correct, could provoke overt hostility and some appalling outrage which would forever mar the occasion in the memory of all gathered there. She who had been in all her trials brave and dignified, would suffer in death indignity and offence.

The Canon heard further cries from inside the house. Father Good looked ill and on the verge of collapse. The door behind them opened. Four young men he assumed were the girl's brothers emerged from the house carrying the coffin at waist level. Behind followed Mr Madden, quiet and unyielding even at this hour. Mrs Madden, flanked by her sisters, stood in the doorway, her hands thrown up in the immemorial attitude of grief. She wept and foam gathered about her mouth. As custom dictated she would not take part in the funeral of her first child to die. Her cries were re-echoed by others outside. Women wept openly. Others though far back in the crowd, extended their hands in hopeless efforts to touch the coffin as though they believed it was sacred.

He moved forward with Father Phelan and Father Good. The crowd parted. Outside the garden gate the men shouldered the coffin and paced slowly behind. In Mill Street the candles in all the window shrines were flickering. In the gathering dim preceding dusk they shone with vivid intensity, creating a memorable image at once both beautiful and poignant. The scarcity of candles, as of so many other essential items, meant the people were sacrificing what for many was their only source of light and for others an important auxiliary source. Though people parted as he approached, the pavements were crowded and they were forced to take to the middle of the road. As they passed some women, their shabby shawls clutched tightly about their bodies and clutching large, brown rosaries in their hands, knelt and dragged their gawking children to their knees beside them. He tried to read the penitential psalms but could not concentrate sufficiently. The sky was darkening swiftly and ominously. Great grey clouds drifted in over the town as if driven by strong winds though there was not even the faintest of breezes. Everything he thought is still, strangely, blackly, unimaginably still. Rain threatened and thunder also. If the coffin was carried on foot all the way to the church they would arrive very late and possibly after night had fallen. At the top of Mill Street he glimpsed a stationary hearse and realised with relief that the coffin would be transferred to it there and the processional cortege would then move at a somewhat faster pace.

They entered Main Street. On all sides the shop windows had their blinds drawn and their doors closed, even if only temporarily. The air was hot and oppressive now. Absorbent, it dulled all sound yet he could hear the low hum of the hearse engine some distance behind and further back, the steady shuffle of feet. They sounded as dreadful as might the roll of muffled drums, or the spaced discharge of a minute gun. He felt weak and sick. Sickened rather than sick. Catherine's long travail was over. She now knew peace and rest and no longer suffered. Of that he was certain. She may not have attained paradise but at least she had attained the peace of death. Yet grief persisted, the sense of loss and more tellingly the sense of betrayal. He would now never know the explanation for the extraordinary phenomenon he had witnessed. He would never know to whom or to what she had spoken and what had evoked such love and adoration in her eyes while that incandescent light shone in her room. Suddenly he realised that he had assumed she had been.

As they entered Church Street he glanced at St. Patrick's above on the heights. Whirling about the solid mass of the building were a series of dense clouds. Like demented furies all in black they swung one way and another as if seeking to destroy it by some demonic powers. Spears of evening sunlight broke through in places, stabbing the staunch, upward-thrusting bell-tower. He gazed in perplexity but firmly told himself that he was paying too much attention to a commonplace meteorological condition.

He whispered to Father Phelan that he was going to mount the steps to the church and that he and Father Good should accompany the cortege around the Castle road which curved gently above the rocky prominence on which stood the church. Some short distance along the Castle road a narrow lane branched off and rose in a slight incline to the church grounds. It made possible the entry of motor cars to the church grounds and was used as a processional route. He was quite undaunted by the steady climb ahead of him. He was exhilarated. It was as if he had shed his debilitating fatigue like a snake reputedly shed its skin: swiftly and painlessly. Nearing the upper flight he turned to watch the funeral below. Never in his life had he witnessed such a throng, even in the emotive years of armed resistence to the British Administration and Crown Forces. He was moved by what he saw. He felt deep gratitude for so vast a tribute so freely given and hoped that the family might draw sustenance from it.

He waited impatiently in the sacristy. He heard the distant patter of rain as it struck the slates of the roof and slantingly, the eastern windows. It steadily increased in strength until it drummed almost defiantly on the roof of the church. He thought that many who had come to the funeral had come unequipped for such a rapid change in the weather. They would be drenched. To his surprise, he was concerned that many might find it prudent to leave the procession and shelter. This he did not want. He needed a multitude at the penultimate ceremony he would conduct for the dead girl. Though the rain pelted down, its fury unabated, he was struck by the silence which persisted despite the loud gush of teeming water. He listened intently like an alert hound scenting quarry. Eventually he heard the steady crunch of footfalls on gravel. The knell commenced its solemn toll. As was traditional, they would shoulder the coffin around the exterior of the church three times. He was, he realised sadly, about to receive her for the last time into the church where she had been baptised and had worshipped. Here she had prayed before the empty tabernacle on Good Friday or before the High Altar in all its Easter splendour. At Christmas she had meditated Christ's birth. In May-time she had venerated Our Lady in prayer and song. Now she would come no more and her lips were forever sealed.

They brought the coffin into the rather cramped mortuary chapel and laid it on a trestle flanked by tall, lighted, amber candles. He glanced at the polished deal boards of the coffin awash with rain. Men soaked to the skin, and women also, crowded in until it was crammed. He began the prayers in latin and then concluded with a decade of the rosary. He found the repetition of the 'Hail Mary' lack-lustre and contrasted it with the quiet regality of Cranmer's prose in the Church of England's Book of Common Prayer which had been his mother's advance choice for her own burial. The responses to the prayers astonished him by their power and volume. He knew the main body of the church, which could hold close on a thousand people, was full. Mr Madden wept openly in the first display of sorrow during his terrible ordeal. Father Good had difficulty containing his emotions. He concluded, blessed himself and hurriedly escaped. He felt new hope. This time he knew it would abide with him forever. She whom he had loved and had sought to serve in the last months of her life would not desert him in death. Nor he her.

The following morning after requiem mass he conducted the burial service and the remains of Catherine Madden, of whom he had known nothing during the greater part of the twenty years of her life, was laid to rest in wet, receptive earth. Remember man, he charged all present, dust thou art and to dust thou shalt return.

8

Thunder rolled in the distance. Sheet lightning flashed across the eastern horizon. He woke to find his bedroom brightly illuminated for a split second, then darkness closed in. He was sweating freely. His nightgown was saturated. He had dreamed that he was back in that nursing home, had relived the long months of isolation there since Catherine's death. He listened and heard nothing but the dying roll of thunder. He had thought he had caught a cry. A lost child. A voice, terrible with that poignancy only the young can suffer. Nothing disturbed the silence of the sleeping household. The house itself seemed cowed and subdued before the ferocity of the storm in progress. He gasped for breath and a restrictive pain tightened about his chest. He rose with difficulty, put on his slippers and dressing gown and, sitting on the side of the bed, he poured himself a tumbler of water from a carafe on the bedside table.

He hungered for a cigarette. He went to the dressing table and rooted about hoping to find some. He found a crushed packet and inside a single broken cigarette. He separated a piece which was not totally broken and then hunted for a match or a lighter. Finding neither he crossed to the bedroom door and, opening it quietly, he passed the grotto erected by Father Good on the landing. A statue of Christ rested on the makeshift altar and about its feet was the usual profusion of flowers. Roses, mostly blood-red and wilting in stagnant water. They aroused his disgust as had the May altar the young man has insisted on erecting as a mark of public devotion. Father Good, he thought morosely was in love with ritual and rubric and would never fully realise what his ordination as a priest entailed.

He had long ago decided that the man was either completely asexual or sexually ambiguous and could remain forever the eternal child, incapable of real transgression, ever innocent. It was that air of simplicity, he reflected, which so aroused his hostility though he could not imagine why.

He continued downstairs and entering the kitchen found there was no need to switch on the light; the curtains were not drawn. The storm was close, the flashes following the claps of thunder with only seconds between. It was near he decided and would soon pass directly overhead. He found a box of matches on the mantlepiece and lit his halved cigarette. Satisfied, he inhaled deeply and felt the cigarette smoke curl about the pit of his stomach. It relieved him only slightly. He sat in a chair and shifted about.

He was ill at ease and at a loss to explain or account for his mood. Thunder storms thrilled rather than frightened him. They had always done so since he was a child. He recalled having seen lightning strike a mighty tree in the grounds of Rathbolgan. It had been cleft apart as if by one stroke of a great axe. The force behind the blow was, he realised, titanic. He rose and wandered about aimlessly. He found himself confronted by the barred front door; he slipped back the bolts and unlocked it. Reaching for his threequarter-length coat he draped it about his shoulders and slipped outside.

The storm was directly overhead and he stood awed as if in the midst of battle. From time to time he could see the church clearly in a flash of lightning. He remained where he was until the storm passed over and began to fade away in the distance. It was followed by a deep vibration that seemed as impacted as the darkness. Rain would soon follow. He considered the wisdom of a short stroll before returning to bed. He heard a cry of distress. Again that ululation he had thought he sensed on waking. Low. Poignant and piercing. He thought it might be a kitten or cat terrorised by the fury of the storm, or one which had strayed from home and was now wild with hunger. He heard it again, plaintive and nerve-racking. It seemed to be a human crying out faintly: "Help me my friend .... Help me ...." Stunned, he realised it was the voice of Catherine Madden, now some months dead.

He was riveted. He saw a light to the left of the church, a beacon which had not been there before. It was bright. Orange-hued. He knew it could only come from the mortuary chapel. Carefully he made his way down the steps and onto the drive. He threw aside his cigarette stub and pulled his overcoat tightly about him. He took infinite care to walk softly and not waken Father Phelan whose room was overhead and who had watched hawk-like for signs of failure or relapse since his long incarceration in the home.

Conscious of his own footsteps he progressed towards the church. He could hear her voice quite clearly now. It sounded as though it came from the cauldron of the earth. Though he had

never in reality heard her speak other than on one occasion —
and then she had spoken only with the greatest difficulty — it he
knew was hers, urgent and infinitely saddening. He reached the
sacristy and using his key gained entry. He hesitated before the
oakgrained door to the sanctuary, fearful of what might lie
ahead. His hesitation was fractional. Bracing himself he entered
and looked inquisitively towards the mortuary chapel which was
on the far side of the gospel aisle, a lean-to off the main building.
Light blazed there and on a trestle lay a coffin. He frowned. No
remains had been received at the church that day, or for some
weeks past.

As he watched the orange glow steadily whitened and grew in
intensity until it was almost blinding. He was dragged unrelenting
towards it. His heart beat with joy. He sensed, felt her presence,
her warmth, her humanity, above all her gentleness as when he
had last held her in his arms. Entranced he moved slowly towards
the mortuary chapel. He saw the coffin was without a lid. He
stared at it perplexed and then he was drawn to it as the moth is to
the flame. Glad expectation was uppermost in his mind. He was
quite without fear. He felt he was about to experience a revelation
of the greatest spiritual importance.

The coffin was full of roses, white and exquisitely scented. He
reached a hand inside and gathered some. They were silken to the
touch and were tinted cream which deepened before his eyes to
the brilliance of polished gold. He gathered an armful and
kneeling held them, calling aloud in his ecstasy: "Catherine,
Catherine, my blessed being, show yourself, bequeath to me your
gift of faith . . . your hope of heaven".

There was a thunderous flash to his left, as if bolt lightning had
struck inside the building. A luminous cloud appeared. It whirled
about and increased steadily in size and volume. As he watched it
began to open out as might the bud of a flower. He saw before
him the incandescent figure of Christ, cloaked in red and hands
parting his white garment at mid-breast, his pulsating heart so
much the focus of his adoration at one time. His face was
beautiful, unearthly, and he radiated love and compassion. Then
he was aware of a figure kneeling in adoration to the right of
Christ. It was his mother in the unspoilt loveliness of her early
womanhood. And to the left knelt the figure of Catherine,
renewed and free of all blemish. He was at first dumbfounded but
recovered and, crying out his praises and adorations, fell to his
knees. Gradually as he watched, the face of Christ darkened
ominously and with a terrible chill he realised that the heart and
hands and feet of Christ were without wound. His countenance

was now vile with hatred and His being radiated nothing but malignancy. He became aware of an overwhelming smell, like that of putrid corpses exposed once more to the light of day.

He screamed, knowing that she, Catherine, like his mother was doomed to perdition. His screeches echoed about the deserted church, on and on like ceaseless waves of terror assaulting a white and silent beach. His wails rose as the figures in the apparitions became more blatantly hideous and obscene. He tore at his face with his hands, trying to reef his eyes from their sockets. He was only dimly aware of hurried footsteps and the lights in the body of the church being switched on. He was suffocating in the foulest of stenches, the smell of evil itself, black, liquid and unspeakably corrupt. He fell to the ground and thrashed about, his body jerking, convulsed. From far off he heard his own cries of horror.

Father Phelan grappled with him but he fought against the restraint. Though far older than the other priest and very much the weaker in constitution, he struggled with the savagery of one possessed of a dark, demonic force. He heard shouted instructions, people running, their shoes striking the tiles of the church floor with irreverent haste and urgency. He opened his mouth wide and like a fanged wild animal sought to seize his captor by the throat. He failed but once his snapping jaw found flesh. He gripped with all his might and bit to the bone. Father Phelan muttered an obscenity and relaxed his hold. He broke free and shrieking in triumph he sought the most distant corner of the church and cowered there, snarling and growling like a cornered beast.

Father Phelan stood some distance from him as if calculating the strength of an animal with which he suddenly found himself confronted. He called quietly, "Canon. Canon", and took a tentative step forward and then less timidly another. Facing the crouched and snarling man, he remained still for a very long time as if lost in contemplation. Eventually with a glance at the raving man he retreated down the aisle towards the sanctuary. The Canon heard the footfalls die away and then as if being entombed, the sound of the sacristy door being slapped and the key being turned. He had, he realised, failed to take the key from the lock after opening it. He was imprisoned. He screamed aloud with renewed vigour. He tore at his hair, felt the skin of his scalp rent apart and the flow of warm blood streak down about his face. He ran to the porch and pounded his fists on the massive front doors of the church, howling: "She is doomed . . . . She is doomed to perdition!" He continued to roar until gradually he was whinneying insanely and spewing forth filth.

Devoid of all strength he sank to the floor and tried to draw some sustenance from the firm, unyielding ground. He heard the arrival of motors as they slid as quietly as possible over gravel. He caught the hum of the engines and then they cut. Car doors were slammed shut. Someone demanded silence. Then he heard the stealthy crunch beneath the feet of people taking great care to move softly. The sacristy door was opened and suddenly he was aware of the stillness. All was uncannily calm, the inviolable silence of the church undisturbed. The glow from the sanctuary lamp was bright, richly, deeply red and it touched everything it shone upon with a soft wine-coloured light. He heard the sound of stealthy steps. The electricity in the body of the church was turned on. He found himself facing a group of people, including Doctor Barrett who approached cautiously. In the background stood Father Phelan and behind him lurked the solid, upright figures of Sergeant Scully and Guard Kinnane. Doctor Barrett inched a little closer. The Canon snarled in terror and alarm and prepared to defend himself. The two Civic Guards circled about until he was threatened on all three sides.

Doctor Barrett tried to reason, to soothe, to deceive. He refused to listen to the soft, culling voice. Suddenly he leaped forward and caught the doctor by the neck. He bared his teeth to tear his throat apart. The Canon toppled him to the ground and was about to gnash down when he got the full impact of an expertly delivered blow at the back of the head. His cry was cut short. He blacked-out.

He felt warm and comfortable, slipping in and out of consciousness. It seemed he was dreaming. Not in sharp, decisive pictures but images which were grey and blurred about the edges. He was being propelled forward through intense darkness. Stars shot against a screen of black and exploded in magnificent showers before falling into oblivion. Gradually he became aware that he was in Doctor Barrett's car. On one side of him sat two bulky figures in dark blue greatcoats. One he vaguely recognised but who he was exactly he could not say. His mind was muddled, he knew it was not functioning properly. There was that warmth, that comfortable, relaxing warmth. He was tempted to sleep and see those stars exploding; suddenly he knew that these stars were rain drops striking the windscreen of the car with uncommon fury. It was raining torrentially. It sounded like a hail of steel drumming incessantly and imperatively on the roof of the car and the bonnet. It hopped off the roadway as though encountering unexpected resistance. Visibility was bad. Only concentration and an unending series of red reflectors set at regular intervals on the road made progress possible. He whimpered softly but could not speak. The man in priest's clothing in the front passenger seat, whom he knew but could not identify, glanced around at him with something akin to pity in his eyes. The Canon stared at him from the back and then looked past him through the windscreen. The gentle rub of the wipers was hypnotically reassuring, as though it was a nursery sound or a rhythm associated with pleasant childhood memories. He lapsed into semi-consciousness and again stars kept exploding before his eyes with a thrilling hiss. Rich, ruby bodies were born in the outer reaches of space, approached rapidly and then disappeared; he felt exhilarated as they grew, desolate and alone as they vanished from sight, simply swept out of existence at the whim of some great, godly hand. Dawn was breaking insipidly when he heard one of the figures, both of whom he realised were in some way custodial, sigh in tired relief and remark, "The city at last, thank God. The asylum's not far from here."

Sun filtered through the drawn blind and everything was bathed in a deep yellow. All was hushed and reassuring. He saw the window-sash was raised a few inches at the base. Small blocks of timber, strategically placed, prevented it from opening any further. The window was barred from top to bottom. They cast shadows in thin, dark strips across the floor and the bed. He tried to guess where he was, to fix himself in time and space, but could not concentrate. Pain, white searing pain, shot through his brain. Involuntarily, he called out. His cry reverberated in the thick-walled room. It eventually died away and all was silent again. An image of himself bound in ropes and gagged with a strip of torn linen flashed across his mind but it was too absurd, too unthinkable to bear any relation to reality. He and that muzzled figure could have nothing in common. He dismissed it and sought to regain his unbroken, restorative sleep. He had hardly succeeded when he was awakened.

A strange man in a dark blue uniform entered to the room with a tray of food. It was a mash of potatoes and vegetables and a small quantity of meat cut in minute pieces as for the infirm, the very ill, the very old. The man fed him from a metal plate and between spoonfuls of food insisted that he drink from a tin mug, draughts of scalding tea, very weak with only the slightest trace of sugar. The man's head was cropped tightly. His eyes were abnormally big and protrusive. His nose dripped continually. He made no effort to use a handkerchief but wiped it on the right-hand sleeve of his jacket which was stained with lines of silver slime like that of snail trails. As he ate he heard a loud scream.

High, it rose to terrifying pitch and continued for some time. There was some shouting, someone roared in reply what obviously was a reprimand of some kind. A heavy door was slammed shut and bolts shut home. Footsteps, loudly aggressive and authoritative, sounded on a stone floor. A ship hooted in the distance. I am close to the sea, he thought.

He tried to recall events. He could remember being bundled into a car and being driven through a continual downpour. It was less a memory, more a sequence of visual images. Prior to that he believed he had been in hell. He had seen it, touched it, tasted it. Silver shards of pain shot across the interior landscape of his mind like sheet lightning flashing over a bleak, desolate waste never inhabited by man or any living thing. He failed to discover who and what he was.

Having finished his feeding, the stranger lay the tray on the floor some distance from the bed as the room was without furniture. He then roughly drew back the bedclothes and turned him on his side. "Fuck you," he muttered loudly, "I knew you'd shit yourself sooner or later. Well you can stay that way until the night staff come on because I'm not wiping your right reverend arsehole." He allowed the patient to tumble onto his back again and pulled the covers up over his body to the level of his ribs. For the first time the man in the bed was aware that his hands were almost ritualistically crossed at his chest and restrained there. He wondered why and how they could remain so but as with the effort to recollect, pain intruded. Blinding agony, excruciating and intolerable.

The man retired, taking the tray with him. He slammed the heavy door behind him and pushed home bolts, top and bottom. The patient tried to assess his position logically. To form in his mind a coherent statement. A sequence of words and imagery with which to explain what was happening. Finally, through trial and error and a difficult process which took a considerable time to formulate, he concluded that he was in the asylum. In a strait-jacket. In an isolation cell. He could not understand why. He saw it as he had so often seen it in reality, the massive bulk of the building as viewed from the banks of the river and which he had always unthinkingly accepted as being part of an otherwise pleasant, silvan landscape. He felt weary. the reason why had no great importance. He wished only to sleep and never wake to the dawn of a new day, the light of another day. He slipped in and out of a state of reverie, a vacancy which he found most agreeable. The great oblong blind which had been mellow orange in colour deepened to indigo, dark blue, and in time black. Darkness he knew had fallen. Traffic sounds of which he had been only faintly aware now grew less intrusive. What could be termed silence settled over the city he knew lay outside the high containing walls of the asylum. Occasionally in the distance someone laughed madly or screamed briefly. The air was heavy with the muted suffering of the other inmates. He heard orders barked in loud, snappish voices and what he thought were children shuffling through leaves under trees which flanked both sides of a country road. The sound suggested autumn, but he could not be sure. The sunlight he had seen earlier in the day had been, he thought, strong summer sunshine. The air had held a sensuous warmth which to him suggested high summer. He was confused. He could not think. He could not imagine. It hurt. It hurt very much to think, deduce. It was so important that he do so yet he resolved to avoid further pain.

He slept, for an eternity it seemed. Then they woke him again. This time there were two men. The faces were bland, impassive, they lacked all interest. They seldom if ever glanced at him directly. Sometimes they scanned his face rapidly and briefly and blinked as though confronted and confounded by a sheet of blank white paper. They helped him from the bed. He was weak and unsteady on his feet. One held him by the shoulders, tightly as though expecting him to take flight. The other stripped the bed and changed the linen. They pushed him towards the corner of the room until he stood within a few inches of it. They then shoved his upper body forward until his forehead rested against the cold, clammy wall. Baring his buttocks they washed away the encrusted bodily waste which had adhered about the anus and along both his upper thighs. They did so quickly, expertly. They probably have to do the likes of this quite often, he thought, but they still have not got used to it. It must rankle to have to clean the soiled flanks of a fellow man.

Finishing their task they returned him to his bed and without speaking either to him or to each other, they withdrew. His buttocks were damp rather than wet. He could readily understand how repulsive he must have appeared to others. As always when awake, like a nagging, persistent pain, lurked the questions: Who am I? Why have I come here? Where have I come from? And always there came the same answer echoing from the distant past and unformulated by him: I have come from hell.

He remained aware for the rest of the night, which was mercifully short, and well into the early hours of the morning. He then lapsed into a comatose-like sleep. Hunger woke him, rather than thirst. His stomach rumbled loudly and he had a dull ache for food. He had been dreaming. Of John. He was sure of that. But the dream had been ugly. Stark, incisive imagery apparently without logical sequence, in vivid, blinding bright colours. What the action was he could not recollect, except that he knew intuitively it had been about John. As always, nightmares of the dead disturbed him deeply, if only briefly. The confusion of dream, imagery and colour gave way to hunger pangs and when he had first opened his eyes the drawn blind was suffused with sunshine. It was, he estimated, about ten o'clock in the morning or later perhaps. He should have been fed by now. He knew where he was. He had realised that some time ago. Now he thought it worthless to carry the quest further and discover why and how he came to be there.

There were three this time, all in the same navy-blue uniforms but now under white coats. With the skeletal build of strong, heavy countrymen, they seemed more suited to toil on the land than to their present jobs as wardens. He knew they were very strong men. They stank of the brutal which was frightening in the dark, nebulous way he could not explain, no more than he could define the fear he felt most mornings on waking and which lurked in a coiled, grey bundle in the corner of his room to the right of the top of the bed. They evoked terror in him by their mere presence and by the long dark shadows they threw across the room; and all the elongated shapes gathered together directly on his body, about his midriff, where they formed a deep pool of liquid horror. Black. Limitlessly, deeply black, more so than one could possibly imagine. Dreadful.

They sat him on the bed and forced his feet into worn slippers. They roughly stuck his arms through the sleeves of a coarse, turquoise dressing-gown. The blue he thought was entrancingly beautiful and seemed to evoke a world where colours existed other than in one's nightmares. They helped him to his feet. One man took him by the arm. He held him in a tight grip which was acutely painful and hurried him forward, compelling him to shuffle quickly in the uncomfortable slippers, while the attendants took long paces such as those in robust health might take on a morning's brisk walk over open heathland or lush, green pastures.

He heard the sea. Distinctly the surf. Not as a heaving mass of turbulent water breaking thunderously against shoreline rocks, but soft, distant, as once he remembered it when as a boy he held a conch shell to his ear and listened to what they assured him was the Atlantic. An image of the ocean presented itself to him. Whole and entire it was more than mere fantasy. It was a clear statement. He saw it. Dark green rather than blue, cold looking. The vast spread of water as remembered from childhood.

He was on a headland looking out on the waves, seagreen and choppy with whitecaps advancing across the swelling surface in irregular fronts. He was on a promontory. Somewhere a lighthouse, brilliantly white, loomed nearby, possibly in the left background. He was not alone. A man. His father. And another man, high-spirited, with a small bowler such as jarvies used to wear clamped on his head of sparse grey hair. He was smiling broadly, showing neglected teeth. His hands were stuck deeply into the pockets of his blue serge trousers. The stance of a relaxed confident man. Across his round waist was strung a gold watch-chain. From it hung gold medals and fobs of all sorts which tinkled rather dully for such a splendid looking metal and which, when catching the sunlight, shone blindingly.

His father wore a suit of white or light tan alpaca. He wore a broad-brimmed straw hat in the Italian style and carried a cane. A black, smooth-surfaced, highly polished stick. With a silver band about its tip and another just beneath its head. The sea. Seagreen. Breaking on the rocks below and the sky above, blue. Very blue. The blue of Mary's mantle or shy, spring flowers. His legs. Bare from the lower edge of his short trousers, which chaffed just above his knees, to the top of his white anklet socks, which were new and kept slipping down at the heel inside his patent shoes. These pumps he disliked wearing because he thought them unmanly with their silver buttons on a strap crossing his upper foot instead of laces. His flesh was covered with pollen as were the legs of his father's trousers. And those of the other man. The rich golden-yellow of buttercups. All around on the clifftop grew tall sedges and sorrel and big daisy-like flowers.

His escort dragged at him roughly. "Come along. Come along, for Christsake. I haven't got all bloody day." He stopped and stared at the man. Rage steadily increased in him. He felt a sickening hatred. His impulse was to strike him a blow in the face. But he could not. If he hit out he would be severely punished. He did not understand how he knew. He just was certain. His anger gave way to loss and hurt. The man had muddied the liquid pool of memory in which he had seen, entrancingly, his father and another man. Somehow, he felt at a very deep level, it was not as trivial as it might seem. That memory of the past, that picture of his father and the other man in the blue serge suit. What was his father? What was his name? He knew his father was that man in white alpaca, carrying a malacca walking cane with a metal inset near the top. Where were they? And why were they there? And what day was it?

Again his escort jolted him. "Come along. I haven't got all fucking day." He resented the man's attitude. Rage again asserted itself. Could the man not see how important the memory was to him? How it might present a vital clue to his identity. To his reason for being here in this strange, implaccably hostile place. He suddenly halted. His mouth slackened and fell open. He listened to the ocean. It was louder this time, less soothingly murmurous than before. He could almost smell the brine and taste its salt on the tip of his tongue. And see the streeling seaweeds waving in the water like banners in a breeze. The attendant tried to pull him forward. He resisted. Stood still. With all his might. Refusing to budge. The man struck him with the open palm of his hand across the face. The stroke had all the power of his squat, solid strength behind it. He cried out. Stunned. He staggered. Almost toppled over but someone behind saved him, catching him roughly by the collar of his dressing gown. The walls were of plastered stone painted a dull deep green. The floor beneath his feet was of uneven, almost rutted flagstones which seemed alive with misery, despair and degradation. He wept bitterly and brokenly. The man dragged him forward. Someone pleaded, "For Jesus sake, Jim, go easy with the decent man." The other snorted, uttered an obscenity and continued to force him on. He again heard the sea. Nearer now. Much nearer. It seemed to be behind a door somewhere to his left. It, he thought, must lead outside. To the ocean. To that headland and the two figures, one of whom was his father. The man in blue called his father James. Almost deferentially, James. And his father called him Paddy in return. Class-consciously. As he would an inferior rarely permitted the privilege of addressing his betters with familiarity; as a person his father would never call mister, except perhaps in cold, cutting anger. And James. His father. Beyond that door. The oakstained one to his left. The kind found in churches or solid, thriving public houses.

There was the sound of approaching feet on stone flags. A key being inserted in the lock and turned. The oak door opened. He barely glimpsed what lay behind. Then it closed. No one came out or went in. But he had seen enough. Inside was a vast room with a high ceiling vaulted in the gothic manner. The floor was of bare boards and the numerous high windows, all were stoutly barred. The walls were a dull, deep chocolate brown. The room was crowded to capacity. Old men in dark suits and loose shapeless jackets. Most wore waistcoats stained heavily with soup or the grease of meat or possibly mucus. Some sported many day's growth of beard, the rest were clean-cut. All their heads had been shaven and their appearance in general was reminiscent of convicts. Many of them showed signs of the deepest inner torment; their faces pinched and drawn, were harrowed in the extreme. Others — sitting on benches by the wall or standing stock still in the middle of the room — were pale faced, their eyes vacant and the spirit within forever quenched, never to be rekindled. Most walked in circles, hands clasped before them or behind their backs. A few who looked frozen held the collars of their jackets tightly closed at the neck with the balled fist of one hand, as if feeling some bitter, sub-arctic winds which they alone could experience. All wore boots. Ugly, unpolished ones of very heavy leather and of stout workmanship. These had no laces, therefore the men were forced to shuffle heavily rather than walk. The stench was appalling. A mixture of bodily odours, dried filth and unmistakably though perplexingly, stale urine. They stank of despair. Terrible, deadening loss of hope. The foulest smell of all. And it was not the sea he had heard. It was not the ocean at all. It was a low moan some occupants of the room were emitting in almost perfect orchestration. On and on it droned, now high, now low, like the chant of the damned. He was stunned. And confused. He thought at first: this must surely be hell. But then he remembered. He had been in hell. It had smelt of roses. Fragile, velvet-leaved roses creamwhite, richly, rarely scented. The attendant who seemed the senior by rank, his self-appointed special keeper, dragged him back.

They stopped outside a white-painted door. He trembled with the fear that he might be about to witness yet another example of men reduced to the level of animals and maintained with the sharpest hostility in a state of outrageous degradation and debasement. The man took a bunch of keys from a clip on his belt and, selecting a pass-key, opened the door. He thrust him forward. To his relief they entered a small yard, immaculately kept. Neatly made beds with crisp, fresh linen and white counterpanes lay spaced evenly along each side. Sunlight streamed through the narrow windows and lay angularly in wheaten hues on the floorboards. A tall, heavily built man who struck him as being rather bullish, red-headed and with heavily brown-blotched skin, stood legs apart at the head of the bed. His hands were stuck into the pockets of his trousers and he affected a rather vicious air of superiority. This man, he told himself, is without mercy. This doctor is my enemy. The man strutted over and asked, "How are you this morning? Feeling any better?"

He stared at the inquisitor in confusion. His voice was light and good humoured but his eyes were bright with malice and ill-disposition. "Up on the bed, Canon, like a good man." His voice was sharp and directive now, all efforts at good nature abandoned. He climbed onto the bed indicated by the doctor and two of the attendants took up positions on either side. They held him, but not tightly, by the feet and shoulders. He heard the door to the ward open and hurried movement as a young and agile person entered. "Sorry, Tom," he muttered under his breath, "got trapped on the way up." He loomed over the patient as he lay in the bed. He was in his mid-twenties. Fair-headed, he wore a college tie held in position by a diamond clip. A signet ring and an emerald in a gold setting on the fingers of his right hand flashed in the morning light. He gazed at the Canon dispassionately for some seconds. "Right," he said aloud to no one in particular. "Will do." Two discs were attached to either side of his forehead. A squat rubber object was inserted into his mouth. "Bite hard on this," the young doctor said quietly. The older red-haired doctor stood at the foot of the bed, his arms folded, his malicious eyes bright and expectant. "Relax, Canon. A split second and it will all be over." He nodded to the younger man who retired behind a screen. There was a click, that of a switch being thrown. Blinding agony shot across the frontal lobes of his brain. His body thrashed convulsively. He cried out and lost consciousness.

Someone shook him roughly by the shoulder. It was the senior attendant. He gave him a mug of tea and told him to drink it. He took the mug but did not drink. Pain still raced across the front of his head. He was in a stupor. Both doctors were now smoking and watching with the studied detachment of men watching a dog trying to catch its tail. The mug of tea was so hot he could hold it only with a determined act of the will. He sipped it slowly, realising that it would be scalding to the tongue. The younger doctor reached a hand into the pocket of his white coat and took out a gold cigarette case which he flicked open with impressive ease. It caught the sunlight and shone with monstrance brilliance. The young man produced a matching lighter and offered him a light. He pulled voraciously on the cigarette and felt the smoke curl comfortably about inside him. He sipped the tea which was strong and well sweetened. He felt very well. Better than he had felt for a long time. There was a totality of body and mind which he had thought he had lost forever. Only the stunning pain across his forehead prevented him from relishing the experience to the fullest. He was watched by the two doctors.

"How do you feel, Canon?" the red-haired man enquired blithely. "A little better perhaps?" He smiled and felt grateful that the doctor should feel concerned about his welfare. He nodded assent. "Good," the doctor replied. "A few more of these and we will have you back with bell, book and candle, prating banalities with the best of them, having knocked the celestial lights out of you once and for all." The younger man snorted with laughter and turned aside to hide the grin. The Canon stared at the older one, aware of his hostility but incapable of comprehending it. The doctor said to the attendants "Right. Shift him back to his cell and send in the next unfortunate."

That man, he thought, hates others, but hates himself far more. The idea formulated itself with conscious effort. He knew he was beginning to think again. Someone took the mug from him. His escort grasped him tightly by the arm as before and led him from the ward. Once outside the senior attendant snatched the cigarette from his mouth and cupping it in his own hand surreptitiously puffed it himself as they retraced their steps down the corridor. The cigarette paper had adhered to the Canon's lip while smoking it. When it had been snatched from him a tiny piece of the flesh had been ripped off. It stung him rawly but did not bleed. He was breathing heavily and staggering, remaining upright only with the greatest of efforts. He heard the sea yet again. Distant and murmurous. They seemed to be approaching it. He halted outside a heavy wooden door and gaped, his mouth slack and dribbling. It lay behind that door. He knew it lay beyond. It roused in him the strong desire to see and smell it and to dabble his hands in the cold, seagreen waters. He babbled irrationally and tried to open the door. The attendant pulled him away and down the corridor. He felt deprivation sweep over him, reducing him to despair. In the cell he climbed readily into bed, wept and then slept and dreamed vividly coloured, unsustaining incidents from the forgotten past.

9

Father Phelan stood at the top of the steps waiting to greet him. His hands were stuck deeply into the pockets of his trousers through slits in the sides of his cassock. His stance was indisputably one of masculine dominancy if not arrogance. Behind him Mrs O'Sullivan hovered uncertainly. Bran yelped and leaping into the air executed a series of complicated movements. Father Good came forward to hold the back door of the hackney car open for him. He grinned sickly while doing so. "You're welcome home, Canon," he said with an air of affected jollity. He nodded his head dully in acknowledgement and edged himself from the back of the car. His feet crunched on the gravel. He winced involuntarily. He had, it seemed to him, been pacing gravelled walks for black centuries behind high containing walls of grey unyielding granite, in a world in which physical and mental ease, colour and warmth was totally absent.

Father Phelan stretched forth a hand, gripping his with unnecessary firmness. The old priest flinched at the grasp. "Welcome home, Canon," he said, grinning broadly. He exuded confidence and an authority his new role as spiritual superior in no way diminished. During the Canon's absence Father Phelan had assumed his duties as parish priest. He was to continue to do so for the foreseeable future. So he was, he knew, here on sufferance. Bound hand and foot, he had been delivered over to those ill-disposed towards him.

"Good God, Canon. You're like a rake. Isn't he, Mrs O'Sullivan? A rake, I declare to God!" Mrs O'Sullivan laughed a high, uncertain laugh like a skittish colt. She came forward, half curtsied and shook hands. She repeated the welcome already extended by the two priests, then she shrank back from him as though he was leprous or in some other way unclean. She had aged considerably and was dressed in mourning. She had had a relative in bad health, he vaguely remembered but the exact details of the kinship eluded him. He refrained from comment.

"We'll feed you up now and have you as fit as a fiddle in no time," declared Father Phelan, his levity of speech in no way reflected in his eyes. "Won't we, Mrs O'Sullivan?" he added, elbowing the housekeeper familiarly. "Indeed we will, Father," she replied. "As fat as . . ." her voice trailed off uncertainly. She blushed under the Canon's cold gaze and turned aside. They stood there like painted figures in a group against the backdrop of the house; or like actors in their allocated positions, waiting for the curtain to be raised so that they could commence their play. Bran, less excited now, lay at Father Phelan's feet, panting, his coat glossy, his extended tongue pink and healthy. In the distance someone discharged a shotgun. There was a raucous scream of crows in nearby trees as, frightened and outraged, they took flight.

Father Phelan's eyes sought his and having established contact held his gaze unswervingly. There was mute triumphant light in them and something dark and malicious about the smile hovering on his lips. "Good God, man, come in, come in. You'll catch your death of cold standing there." He took him by the arm with undue licence and half-helped, half-hurried him up the steps of the house where he had once been master. Sometime. A grief, an eternity ago. "We have a grand fire in the room for you and Mrs O'Sullivan has cooked a chicken, and if all that isn't enough, Docotor O'Malley handed in a brace of wild duck. Man dear, there'll be no end to the feasting and rejoicing the prodigal son having returned." He ushered him into the hall and Mrs O'Sullivan took his greatcoat, and Father Good his biretta and breviary which he found himself holding tightly in his right hand.

They entered the sitting room where a fire, a mixture of wood and well hardened peat was blazing. "A drink, Canon, before you have your dinner. Sherry perhaps, or some of the hard stuff?" Malice was rampant in his eyes. Mockery tinged his voice. He declined Father Phelan's offer. "Ah well," said Father Phelan, "time enough for that. We'll bide our time until Mrs O'Sullivan calls us. Sit down, man. Sit down and get a heat of the fire. You look perished with the cold. Perished altogether."

He took the armchair indicated, that to the left of the fire and usually given to visitors, the chair opposite by tradition being reserved for the head of the household. Father Phelan took possession of it now with some glee. He sat on the edge, legs splayed apart, hands clasped warmly. He was hugely humoursome and forthcoming, smiling from time to time as if privy to some mystery, some trivial secret which nevertheless afforded him considerable pleasure. He turned to Father Good who hovered about the doorway. "Come in, boy, come in and for

God's sake, close the door or we'll all end up frozen stiff." Father Good took a seat on the settee directly in front of the fire.

"It's terrible weather altogether, Canon," Father Phelan continued. He reached forward as if to emphasise his words. "I'll tell you something, believe me or not. The birds of the air are falling to earth, frozen to death. Trees that have lasted for centuries in Lord Bernard's estate are being killed overnight by the frost. Blasted to death. We have our work cut out for us there's been so many dying with the cold. Old people mostly, God help them. Four to my knowledge have been found dead in their beds for lack of warmth. Of course we're doing all we can to mitigate their suffering. The members of the Society of Saint Vincent de Paul are out day and night, doing what they can in the face of hazardous weather conditions unexperienced for at least three hundred years."

He paused as if awed by the immensity of his statement. He wiped his spittle-flecked lips with the back of his hand. "The ground in the graveyard" he continued, "is frozen solid. Like a rock, or so Paddy Killeen tells me. He had to take a pick-axe before he could open up a grave. Frozen to a depth of over two feet he said and I believe him; whatever the man is or isn't, he isn't a liar."

He paused and reflected shortly. His face assumed the mask of tragedy. "Of course Canon, it's no coincidence that just a hundred years ago to this very year we had the famine and our people died by the thousands on the roadside with nothing in their bellies but grass and inedible foliage. People dropping down dead for want of food while, the great O'Connell himself testifies, ships laden with wheat and butter and the grain products of our rich land sailed daily from Irish ports for destinations in England. Their life's blood and sweat wrung out of them by the intruder." His voice took on a bitter determination of surprising ferocity. "We won't forget, Canon. We won't forget. And that's what makes us what we are. We kept faith, thank God, and please God we always will. Don't you agree, Canon?"

There seemed little to agree upon. He had followed the spate of speech only with great difficulty. He nodded tiredly. He found the heat of the fire suffocating and the company of the two priests tiresome. He decided to escape. He rose abruptly to his feet. "I would very much like to go to my room if you do not mind, Father. I feel tired after the long journey and somewhat debilitated generally." His voice trailed off as the insincerity of his speech struck home. Father Phelan immediately appeared concerned and adjusted his facial expression accordingly. "Of course, Canon, of course. Why not lie down for a while? I'll have Mrs O'Sullivan keep a dinner hot for you. Perhaps a little later in the evening you'll chance a bite or two." He whispered hoarsely: "She worked like a nigger trying to get everything right for your homecoming. Take it a little later, just to please her."

"Very well," he relented. "But perhaps before that a cup of tea. I feel rather thirsty."

"To be sure, I'll escort you to your room and see that you get a good mug of hot, sweet tea. There's a grand fire lit above for you, thanks to the grace of God and the cunning of Jack Deasey the coal merchant. He said he'd see you right for the winter, for all that gold is easier to come by than coal. Black gold he calls it and he's not far out."

Father Phelan entered the bedroom and beckoned him to follow. Bran trotted in and promptly crouched by the new master's feet. Father Phelan stood still like the sole but staunch defender of a threatened position in a line of battle. "It's a bit crowded at the moment, Canon. I had to clear your study. You know how short of space we are. These old books and things can go up to the attic if you still want to keep them, but they can't remain down here taking up valuable space. I don't suppose they're of any great value." His voice was heavily sardonic.

The Canon gazed at the books stacked about the room in untidy confusion. Virtually all his personal possessions had been removed from his study downstairs and piled up with a total lack of concern for his feelings or any wishes he might harbour as to their ultimate value. He felt as if confronted with the dross of his life. "No, Father," he said tiredly, "there is nothing of any importance here. You may dispose of them as you wish."

"Good," Father Phelan exclaimed, "I'll see to them then. It'll make your room more comfortable and if you prefer to dine alone we can always arrange for you to take your meals here." His tone was more dictatorial than simply suggestive. "Thank you, Father. That might be wisest and the least burdensome to all concerned. Now if you forgive me, I have a headache — the travel — the excitement ..." Father Phelan beamed expansively, "Say no more. A nod is as good as a wink to a blind horse. And don't worry about attending mass unless you feel in form for it. These things take time and who knows but you might be back saying mass yourself in your own good time." Father Phelan patted him on the shoulder as one might a dog.

He sighed and subsided gratefully into an armchair. In the grate a feeble fire glowed in spartan heroism. It yielded a little warmth for which he was grateful. He drew a packet of cigarettes from his pocket with effort as his hands were disfigured with ugly, split chilblains which were wrapped in bandage under the protection of his mittens. The simple process of lighting up was very intricate and caused some pain. Having extracted the packet he opened it and offered one to the younger man who declined. He searched in his coat for a box of matches. He managed to find one and, his hands trembling, struck one and lit a cigarette. He smiled apologetically at Father Phelan who stood looking at him in cold dispassionate hated and who had not made the slightest effort to assist him. He drew in avidly with all the intensity of a heavy smoker. His fingers were stained with nicotine, the index and second one of his right hand heavily so. He pulled out a handkerchief to wipe his forehead but realised it was stained and grubby. He hastily returned it to his pocket.

"You're alright then?" Father Phelan enquired coldly. "Yes, yes, Father," the Canon hastened to assure the man. "Quite well, thank you, and thank you indeed for all your kindness." His face glacial, the younger priest muttered, "I'll have you jumping through hoops, Canon James Fitzgerald, before I'm finished with you. I'll have you jumping through rings like a trained mongrel in Duffy's circus." His face screwed up with hatred he stared at the dejected figure in the chair and then calling Bran, he left the room. The dog obediently followed.

The old man stared at the fire, unable to believe that the priest had spoken as he had. Perhaps, he told himself, he was mistaken. With his nerves stretched to the utmost and strained beyond normal endurance he may well have imagined the last words. Tired, he lay back secure in the headwings of the chair. He tried to think, to bring the bewildering events of the last few days into sharper focus and better perspective but failed utterly to place the confusing imagery into proper sequence.

His mind slipped back to where he had been a few days ago. The room had broad high windows which overlooked the valley and the river which flowed downstream towards the harbour some miles away. The far side of the valley rose steeply and was undefiled by human dwelling. Well established trees were scattered across its rich, green pastures. From the window of a small private room he had an even better view and liked to sit in an armchair, a shawl draped across his shoulders and a blanket about his knees, and watch the nightly departure of the mailboat for England, its decks crowded with people waving to those on shore. He thought it odd, this strange compulsion of people on shore to wave as they watched the boat sail down river. People halted, he noted, and smiled broadly as if to hearten those on board. For some weeks a young schoolboy in uniform had cycled furiously along the road which ran parallel with the river for some miles. He had begun to look forward to the boy's arrival and his furious efforts to keep up with the smoothly moving boat. Then, for some unaccountable reason, he had stopped coming and in time he came to think of him almost as a dream figure. There was a desperation, a poignancy and a certain bravery about those on board the boat who waved frantically in return though they were going into exile. Most were country people from all over the southern counties. Strong, big-boned men and handsome dark-haired women with the fine broad hips much sought after by farmers intent on marriage because they indicated easy, capable childbirth. Exile, he thought bitterly. Servitude on building sites, or in thrall to the lower-middle classes with social pretensions who had no idea of how to treat a serving girl with decency. Many he knew would end up in factories working day in and day out to send home a pittance. The women would return home powdered and permed, having bartered their natural beauty for a cheap fashionable idea of what constituted beauty. Crimped and painted and affecting high, nasal, English accents.

There had been nuns in that home, if home it was. White-robed nuns who clattered about on the floors of polished wood, their strides authoritative and aggressive, as intimidating and bullying as their tongues. Ungracious, he thought, was how best to describe them. Hard, glinting eyes. Bitter, black, tight-lipped mouths. Not that they had been unkind to him. No, not unkind. But then he could not recall one act which had not derived from their unspontaneous, dehumanised, Christian sense of duty. However, for all its faults it had been a vast improvement on the other place, the asylum with its lost souls haunting the open wards or shuffling about endlessly in circles in the men's dayroom. Spent, lifeless hulks.

Mrs O'Sullivan entered with a tray on which rested a large mug and a plate of plain biscuits. She lay them beside him on a low table which had never been part of the bedroom furniture in his time. "It's grand to have you back, Canon. God bless you, but you look the picture of health. With the help of God you'll be back to your old self in no time at all." She fussed about him, chattering loudly and with obvious pleasure. He adjusted the blanket quite unnecessarily draped about his knees and the shawl about his shoulders. "If the cold spell breaks at all, you'll be able to go for a grand walk to keep you occupied. Out to Castle Bernard you should go and walk about the estate, it's a picture of paradise itself, it's that beautiful. There isn't anything else you would like?" He shook his head. She patted him fondly on the shoulder. "The poor hands are at you again I see. We'll have to do something for them or you won't be able to say mass again." She paused, knowing she had said the wrong thing. The colour drained from her face, her eyes showed concern and some sorrow. She blushed then recovered herself. Laughing dismissively she said, "You're sure you don't need anything? Father Good left a whole pile of cigarettes, two hundred in the top drawer of the chest over there. Don't let on you know who they're from or he'll have my life." She stood some seconds, hands aflutter and then, smiling broadly, left him.

The view from his window was not very exciting. The garden was directly below and beyond stood the protective screen of trees planted some sixty years before. They had developed well and had a quiet elegance even in their winter starkness. Not without interest, he thought, but altogether incomparable with the view of the river and road seen from the window of his room in the home. He missed the continuous traffic on the low road and the passage of ships, particularly the mailboat to and from the city quays further upstream.

His days became a grey blur of activities fading indistinguishably into one another, until he could no longer tell the difference between the days and weeks and even months. He ate, he excreted and he slept. On waking he ate and again excreted and slept again. The days he spent largely on his own by the meagre fire for which he was so grateful. Father Good and Mrs O'Sullivan had made tentative efforts to engage him in topical conversations from time to time but evoking no response they no longer tried, though both made a point of calling to his room morning and evening for some polite, stilted exchanges. Father Phelan rarely if ever, visited him. Imperceptibly the hard winter softened and spring arrived. The seemingly dead earth and its dormant life asserted themselves; Guard Mullins came to turn the soil he had broken last November for the winter frosts to work upon, and prepared to plant and sow.

He ventured out into the garden and derived a sense of peace and well-being from strolling in the sunshine on the southern walk by the high stone wall tufted with valerian and wild snapdragons. He meandered up and down oblivious of Guard Mullins. Occasionally it struck him that he had once been deeply grieved, but for whom he could not now remember. He tried very hard to recall but such effort resulted in searing agony which shot through his brain in the painful flashes he had come to dread. He sought the refuge of his room. Hardly had he settled in his chair than Father Phelan came bustling in, apparently in high spirits.

"Wouldn't you think of taking your meals with us, Canon?" he suggested in a tone which intimated very much more than mere suggestion. "Mrs O'Sullivan is getting on. Save her old trotters, and her heart if it comes to that." He stood above him smiling frostily.

"I'd rather not if you don't mind. Not just yet. Sometime in the near future perhaps."

Phelan snorted. "Ah, what's the matter with you, man. We'll ate the mate and praties and not yourself." He laughed harshly: "There's not a pick on you. We'll have to do some fattening up on you before you'd be ready for the pot!"

He knew it was not meant as a joke. It was rank hostility and bad manners. He winced and closed his eyes. The man had no idea what horror the suggestion conjured up in his mind. "Please, Father. I am very tired."

"Maybe you are, Canon, but you can't expect to be waited on hand and foot for the rest of your life. The poor woman downstairs is worn out with the work she has without taking care of a chronic invalid. If I had any idea things would be like this I would never have agreed to the Bishop's suggestion that we take care of you instead of shoving you into a hell-hole of a nursing home, or an asylum if it comes to that. Why don't you get out more, man. Meet people. Assert your will-power. When the entire lump of fat is boiled down, it's only a matter of will-power."

He sighed, "I will try, Father. I will try. I agree I must be a burden to everyone, Mrs O'Sullivan most of all."

"Good man yourself." Father Phelan patted him playfully on the back. The old priest was about to protest when he realised that was exactly what his tormentor wished. What was it he had said? 'I'll have you jumping through hoops before you know where you are, Canon James Fitzgerald.'

The next day there was no fire in the grate when he returned to his room after a stroll. Mrs O'Sullivan, greatly embarrassed explained that Father Phelan had given instructions that it was not to be lit in future. He nodded dully as she placed a jar of evergreens in the fireplace, saying without too much conviction that it would liven the place up. He thanked her for her kindness as she put before him a pot of tea and china on a tray. She explained that she had left him a cold dinner on the table in the kitchen, seeing the day that was in it, and asked if he didn't mind too much because it was only for this once. He reassured her that it did not matter at all. A cold dinner would do very well on such a

warm, sunny day. Stumbling somewhat, he again thanked her
and settled down to have a cup of tea. Mrs O'Sullivan left close to
tears. Soon the house had the unmistakable air of being deserted.
He sat gazing at the fronds in the fireplace.

Some time later he roused himself from his stupor and decided
to take a walk. He made his way downstairs carefully. He passed
through the kitchen. Bran lay sprawled in front of the range
which was lit. It radiated heat. Meat was being cooked in the
oven. The dog glanced curiously at him and then, stretching
himself contentedly, resumed his former position. In the garden
he sought the shade of the trees. The sunshine was strong and the
day very warm. He felt cold yet could not tolerate the open,
burning light which, apart from other things, proved too harsh
for his eyes. He paced the path totally absorbed but quite without
conscious thought. Faintly he heard organ music and then the
sound of trumpets in ascent. Soon the sound of hymns being sung
out of doors drifted towards him like the scent of an unseen
flower. The notes rose and fell as if a soft breeze was blowing. The
voices varied. Now close, now piping and distant. An image
flashed across his mind. That of a young and beautiful girl
dressed in blue and veiled in white. She was young and expectant
as only youth can be. She was without sin. Wholly innocent in a
striking manner. He felt, briefly, pain. Intense hurt coupled with
sorrow and longing. He was drawn to the music as if by some
strange but undeniable compulsion.

He walked to the upper half of the garden, towards the gate
into the church grounds where it seemed the music and singing
originated. It was stoutly boarded and, from close examination of
the lock and chain, recently padlocked. He tugged at the heavy
chain and tried in vain to wrench off the padlock. It had, he knew
instinctively, been put there to confine him within the grounds of
the presbytery. He stood waiting as, like the music, the vision of
the young girl faded on the still, warm air. Suddenly he thought of
the house. He could get out through the front door. He hurried
inside and found to his relief that the kitchen door was unlocked
and he could enter the hall. His heart was beating rapidly as he
passed along the passage. He felt possessed of a fierce energy,
elemental and driving him on blindly. He felt he had to discover
what that picture meant and why it aroused such grief in him. The
exit was locked. He cried out in desperation. He tried to enter the
study and the sitting room, both of which would have allowed
him to get out through the window with only a small drop to the
ground. Both were locked. The keys were missing from the locks.
He stood still, dismayed. The side windows of the kitchen and the

pantry were barred, as was the window of the laundry room. He
had no means of escape. Someone, undoubtedly Father Phelan,
had taken great care to see that he could not leave the house or
garden.

He returned to the hall door and stood there, looking at it
dazed and unable to think. He stared at its glaring whiteness
which hurt his eyes. Agony ripped from the base of his spine and
shot the length of his back, striking the top of his head with
stunning blows. He screamed and lapsed into darkness. He came
through to find himself sprawled on the floor.

Distantly he heard singing. Tremulous and rather what one
might imagine spirit music to be. He saw the young woman in the
blue dress again. Her white silken stockings, white patent shoes
and veil simply and very becomingly draped upon her head. She
was in a group of women and young girls dressed as she was.
They moved forward at a processional pace. All carried sheets of
music and her voice was raised, as was theirs, in praise. In the
background towered an immense warehouse, its whitewashed
facade draped with lengths of red and white material. The breeze
caught her veil and seemed about to whip it off. She laughed
delightfully and sought to keep it in place. He recognised
Catherine Mary Madden. Suddenly he knew who he was, where
he was and where he had been all these years.

He rose uncertainly to his feet and went upstairs to his
bedroom. He opened a wardrobe with a full length mirror on the
inside of the door and gazed at his reflection for the first time in
many years. He had aged. His hair had been chopped rather than
cut. It was wild and he had no doubt, filthy. His stock was dirty
and in places green with age. His soutane was no cleaner and his
boots, without laces as they had been in the asylum, were
unpolished. On impulse he entered Father Phelan's room. It was
neat and comfortable. Both the windows were open top and
bottom in this airy room. Their white lace curtains wafted gently
in an almost imperceptible breeze. He could hear the song clearly
now and recognised it as being eucharistic. It was, he realised, the
feastday of Corpus Christi when the host was carried in a gold
monstrance, with all the pomp and ceremony the parish could
muster, through the streets of the town below. At one time such
outward displays of Irish faith had been proscribed by the ruling
ascendancy, as they were now called. He had always known that
there was consequently an element of the vengeful in this
impressive display of reverence to the host beneath its canopy of
cloth-of-gold.

He glanced through the window. His view was somewhat

obscured by nearby trees but through a gap he had a good view of the steps from the church down to the street below. Flags flew from every possible position. The pale gold and white of Vatican City with its papal coat-of-arms and elsewhere the plain red and white flags generally accepted as being in the colours of Christ the King. In some instances the national tricolour of green, white and orange was flown and doubtless there were a few blue and gold flags from the nineteen-thirty-two Eucharistic Congress, which had been held in Dublin, flying from some windows. Bunting was everywhere. It criss-crossed the flights of steps, as it did Church Street and all other streets through which the procession would wind its way. An escort of military officers in full dress uniform and with drawn steel swords he remembered would flank the monstrance-carrying priest and those red-sashed men who bore the canopy of gold. Away to the north-west he could see the dull, concrete back of the convent and the nearby schools. Nuns in sun absorbing black clustered around a short flight of steps which led to a glass-enclosed porch. One or two of these women were in white. Postulants, he thought, and marvelled at the wonder of regaining the simple faculty of remembrance. The nuns, who were an enclosed order and therefore could not participate in the day's events, traditionally gathered there to witness, if even at a distance, the Benediction of the Blessed Sacrament which took place on the first terrace before the statue of the Virgin and Child. Both figures, he recalled, were crowned and two of the right-hand fingers of the infant-in-arms, which were raised in benediction, were broken by some witless vandals in the past. He himself had always reserved the privilege of conducting the brief service and imparting the solemn benediction with the gold enclosed host. Now, he thought bitterly, Father Phelan had usurped his position as he had in so many other things. The charge he knew to be untrue since he was not sufficiently well to conduct the service. Nevertheless it rankled. He listened carefully. He could not hear any singing. The procession, he calculated, had not reached South Main Street or passed the renamed Orange Hall by Kilbrogan Hill. He had plenty of time in which to make preparations to receive Father Phelan on his return to the house.

He went upstairs to the bathroom and, running the taps, filled the bath. Watching the steam rise, he could not recall when last he had taken a bath. He had disliked it on the few occasions he thought it imperative, and had remained in the water only as long as was necessary to scrub himself thoroughly. He undressed and found that his body was in no way unclean. Someone, he realised, supervised this basic hygienic measure as they did his shaving.

Father Phelan, he guessed, as he immersed himself in the hot water, or possibly the nursing sister Doctor Barrett had arranged to attend him in his first illness some years ago. Within a few minutes he rose and stepping out of the bath dried himself with a rough but serviceable bath-towel from the airing cupboard on the landing. He shaved what he estimated was about three days growth on his face and then washed his hair. He took his time and, characteristic of his old self, he took infinite pains about each stage down to clipping and trimming his toenails. Finishing, he went to his room and changed his clothes completely. Whoever might be responsible for his wild and unkempt state in the past, it certainly was not Mrs O'Sullivan, he thought as he surveyed his wardrobe with its clean soutanes and suits and his chest-of-drawers with its ample supply of clean linen, underwear and carefully folded shirts. Completing his attentive dressing, he inspected himself in the mirror. He was in all outward respects a new man. Only the ravished face, the eyes, hinted at his past ordeal. The approaching sound of voices raised in song steadily grew stronger, more distinct. It was passing up Main Street and would soon turn into Church Street where he could view it from one of the windows in Father Phelan's bedroom. Satisfied that he was presentable, he went downstairs to the kitchen where he made a pot of tea and subsequently enjoyed a cigarette as he awaited the arrival of the procession. He experienced hatred for the two priests whom he considered responsible for what he now regarded as forcible imprisonment.

The singing grew steadily nearer until it was obvious that the children in the vanguard had arrived on the uppermost terrace before the temporary altar. The boys would be in their 'good' first holy communion suits, the girls in their white dresses and veils. Each would carry a bamboo cane with coloured pennants at the top. On seeing the canopy enter Church Street below, they would hold them aloft in homage to the host and they would break into a zestful hymn. It suddenly occurred to him that the meat in the oven was for the military guests Father Phelan would be entertaining after the procession. The commander of the small garrison stationed in the town for the duration of the war would, as was customary, dine with the priests, as would one of the junior officers serving as guard-of-honour. It was a civilised and polite way in which to mark the gratitude of the parish to those providing the military escort and trumpeters who heralded the elevation of the host during High Mass before the procession and again at the blessing of the multitude.

He lit another cigarette and patiently waited. Eventually he heard the children burst into song and knew that the climax of the day's excessive proceedings was fast approaching. He decided to remain where he was rather than watch the ceremony from Father Phelan's room. He heard the barked command to present-arms, then a peal of trumpets which rang thrillingly on the warm, still air. There was a pause and eventually the litany commenced. It was soon followed by the hymn which brought the ceremony to a close. The host would be placed in a pyx and would be carried back to the tabernacle of the high altar in a less splendid procession. He heard the sound of gravel being displaced as someone hastened around the house to the side entrance. He stiffened and then relaxed. It would be Mrs O'Sullivan rushing to prepare the dinner for the guests. He heard her insert a Yale key into the lock and apply the slight pressure necessary to open the door. She called him anxiously, rather like someone calling a much loved cat which had the infuriating tendency to stray for many hours. He rose and went out into the hallway to greet her. She stared at him in astonishment, dropping a small red purse which contained her house key, some loose small change and her rosary beads. The contents spilled all over the hallway. She made no effort to retrieve them. She looked at his face anxiously and then stared at his clothing. "Canon!" she muttered aghast.

He glared hard at her though not with ill-intent. The woman had played no part in the blatant attempt to usurp his authority. Whatever she may have done, she had been compelled to do it on orders. Her position left her no choice. An aging woman, she could not expect to obtain a job anywhere else. She depended on Father Phelan for food and shelter in her old age, and any other benefits he might see fit to confer on her. She would have to comply with his wishes.

He picked up the scattered contents of her purse, replaced them carefully and handed it back to her. "Please open the dining room, Mrs O'Sullivan, and the sitting room."

She poked about in the shallow pockets of her fashionable coat, into which she had wedged the awkward keys to the rooms. She fumbled in what she realised was terror. She failed to insert the key into the lock of the dining room.

"Allow me," he said, taking it from her and turning it, he opened the door. Ignoring the woman who was obviously considering flight at the first opportunity, he entered the room. Everything was prepared as if for a feast. The parochial silver and antique Waterford glassware were neatly arrayed on the table which was covered by two heavy damask linen cloths that did not quite match. One had a pattern of creamwhite roses and winged angels supporting shamrock and entwined harps; the second, which was of a richer white, showed round-towers and Banba with her Irish wolfhounds. Unlike the other, it was trimmed with delicate lace. On the fine, highly polished mahogany sideboard — its surface protected by a commonplace strip of linen, but an opulent piece of furniture by any standards with its silver patterned design faintly superimposed on the glass doors — stood a number of silver and porcelain dishes covered in light, slightly dampened muslin to keep the food fresh. Nearby was arranged an impressive array of spirits and, cooling in a plated silver container, some bottles of wine immersed in ice. The man never knew what a bathroom was for until he entered the diocesan seminary, he thought viciously, and look, here he is, chilling choice wine for his guests.

"Very impressive, Mrs O'Sullivan. I hope you had some help with all these preparations?" She coughed nervously. One hand touched her throat. "Yes, Canon. My sister Hannah's eldest one, Sissy, came over and gave a hand. I'm expecting her at any minute to help with the serving. As skinny as a rake, Canon, but a great worker. Great altogether. You'd think she was one of Beamish's brewery horses, she's that strong and willing." She paused and again her hand fluttered about her throat. Then she said in a soft, shy voice "Poor Hannah, the grand woman that she was, died a few years back and left a big family to be cared for. But she died a happy death, thanks be to God."

He did not remember the woman. He believed they had never met but felt some remark was called for. "I'm sorry to hear that. Very sorry indeed. And her husband and children? They are, I hope, well?"

"Thriving, Canon. Thriving altogether. God is good," she said, "God is good." Now avoiding the woman's gaze, he asked quietly but firmly: "Was I ever harsh or brutal — even violent perhaps — in all my years of illness?" Mrs O'Sullivan replied without hesitation and with what he thought of as great kindness "Indeed you were not. You were as gentle as a lamb but away in a world of your own. You never raised as much as a little finger to anyone or lost your temper either." She paused and, speaking in a rush, she added: "It's great to see you back to your old self. Thanks be to the living God."

His emotions were roused. Tears came to his eyes. He tried to disguise them by speaking coldly. "Thank you, Mrs O'Sullivan. Now the sitting room if you would, please."

She found the key and inserted it without any difficulty. He stepped inside. Incongruously a fire of logs blazed in the fireplace.

The heat was sweltering. "I think we had better open those windows, Mrs O'Sullivan. Can you possibly manage them?"

"Of course I can. Haven't I my old stick?" Her tone was happy and seemed to grow lighter all the time. The woman is quite pleased that I have to some extent regained my health, he thought in amazement. She took a long stick rather like a broom handle with a hook attached to the top. With it she expertly undid the window clasps and the anti-burglary devices attached to each window. She opened both, top and bottom. Fresh air wafted into the room. "Thank you, Mrs O'Sullivan. That will be all for now. And I would prefer if you didn't discuss me or my health with anyone before I can speak to them myself." His voice was grim, underscored with bitterness. She looked sadly at him and then said gently, "Of course not, Canon."

She left and he strode to the window. He heard the boisterous voice of Father Phelan raised in good-humoured banter with another man whose voice was deep, well modulated and had an unmistakable air of command about it. He also recognised the nervous, high-pitched sounds of Father Good talking with someone. Conversation, he reminded himself, was not one of Father Good's strong points. He could not hear the accent of the person to whom he was speaking. There must be four of them and all strode heavily on the drive.

Father Phelan's tirade rang out with characteristic bluntness. "Still and all, it must be a mighty slap in the face to them to see the consecrated host, flanked by a guard-of-honour of the National Army, carried through the streets of a town in which it was forbidden for centuries for a catholic to as much as bless himself publicly. Oh, I saw the gang of them in the Allen Hall. The Allen Hall, I ask you! The old Orange Hall that used to be, and they peering out, for all the world like spies, as the procession passed. And I thought to myself, as my mother used to say, you never thought you'd live to see the day." The splenetic voice broke into harsh laughter. It was patent that during the Canon's illness the younger priest had lapsed into the broad, common accent of the eastern extremes of the country where he was born. "God is good. Many an Irishman's bones rest easier in foreign soil now that we have our independence and the Catholic Church is safely enthroned in the heart of the Irish. Well, the good Irish at any rate." What was meant as a witticism failed to impress those in his company. There was no responsive laughter and an uneasy silence fell.

Someone rang the doorbell. Mrs O'Sullivan hurried to open. There was a loud exchange of greetings. Father Phelan waved towards the stout figure of his housekeeper. "The good woman herself. Sure where would we be without her and her superb culinary skills, which are about to be revealed to all and sundry." His banter ceased abruptly. There was an awkward pause, followed by the sound of someone hurrying down the hall.

Father Phelan entered the room and addressed him. "Ah, Canon, yourself!" He closed the door, then turning to face him, paled. "You're feeling alright, Canon. I mean you're ..." He faltered and lapsed into silence.

The Canon stared coldly at the spluttering man for some seconds. He was balder than before and carried himself with all the smugness of a fat-bellied bishop or some more senior ecclesiastic. His face and features had subtly changed. The almost perpetual sneer of the poorer farming class was there as was the hard glint of malice. The Canon sought his barb and aimed it with devastating effect. "I am not quite jumping through hoops like a trained mongrel in a circus, if that is what you mean, Father."

Father Phelan frowned deeply, attempted to speak but floundered and fell silent. "I think, Father, you will agree it would be impolite to keep our guests waiting."

Father Phelan recovered somewhat. "Canon, it might be best if I were ..."

The old man interrupted him. Striding to the window, he gazed absently at the scene outside and spoke with subdued ferocity. "I gather, Father, that our superior, His Lordship the Bishop, placed the responsibility of administering this parish on your shoulders during my ... indisposition. Correct me if I am wrong."

"You are quite right, Canon."

"However, he at no time appointed you or anyone else my guardian in law?"

"No, Canon. He did not."

His voice was cold with fury as he spoke. "Then please note that I am resuming my duties as parish priest and will in time seek the approval of the Bishop. Unless of course you intend contesting it on any grounds?"

Father Phelan seemed about to argue though for what reason it was impossible to say. He refrained. "No. I don't intend opposing your wishes in anything. I'm glad to see you have recovered your good health."

The Canon drew a short breath and experienced a feeling of vengeance he knew to be basically mean and contemptible. "Thank you, Father. And now, our guests. I feel it would be churlish to keep them waiting any longer. Please show them in."

"Of course." Father Phelan swallowed with difficulty then swiftly left the room and hurried along the hall.

A pause followed during which he surmised that Father Phelan was quietly issuing a note of caution. Then clearly and audible his voice was raised to carry: "My apology for keeping you waiting, gentlemen, but the Canon himself is with us, happily need I say, and would like to receive you himself."

He turned and braced himself for their entrance. Father Good came first. He had gained weight and his face was full and melon-shaped. His eyes were dark, those of a perpetually discontented person. He regarded his superior for some seconds and then hastened forward. Sinking to one knee he reached for his hand and kissed it impulsively, uttering a faint cry of distress. The Canon felt revolted by the gesture and longed to shove the kneeling figure from him but knew that generosity and sincerity had impelled the young man to act as he did. He raised him and embraced him stiffly but affectionately. Father Good, he sensed, had realised the true nature of his sexuality and was being racked by the knowledge. The young man turned away and as if seeking shelter, went to the window and with head bowed, struggled to regain control of his tumultuous emotions.

A dark-haired young officer of prepossessing handsomeness, charm and gentleness followed. He bowed slightly and extended his hand. "Lieutenant Doyle, Canon. Delighted to meet you. I don't believe I've had the pleasure before now." The lieutenant then went over to Father Good and succeeded in engaging him in light conversation, much to the young priest's relief and pleasure.

A senior officer, whom he recognised instantly but whose name he failed to remember and whom he had entertained in the past, now entered, the epitome of joviality and heartiness.

"Splendid to see you, Canon. Simply splendid." His voice was oddly impersonal and clipped, more befitting an English officer than a soldier of the Irish Army, as was his neatly trimmed moustache, his tightly cropped grey hair.

"Commandant O'Kelly, I believe," and he felt the man take his hand in an unnecessarily firm clasp.

"In person. In person I have to admit," and the man scanned his face in close scrutiny.

Father Phelan entered the room and stood at the back of the small gathering looking somewhat at a loss. The Canon turned to him. "I'm sure our guests would like something to drink before dinner, Father. Why not offer them something from our excellent supply."

The sarcasm was not lost on the curate who flushed deeply, nor

on O'Kelly who raised an eyebrow quizzically and smiled faintly
with his lips: "Splendid idea. A small Irish for me, if you'll forgive
me for drinking spirits at such an ungodly hour of the day and
before we partake of what I know from past experience is going to
be a simply splendid meal. But the heat, y'know, the heat."

The lieutenant requested a tonic, as did Father Good. He
himself demanded white wine. Father Phelan brought up the
drinks from the dining room, served them diligently and indeed
generously. The commandant raised his glass in toast: "Your
very good health, Canon. Your very good health." All raised
theirs in response and sipped their drinks politely.

"Are you not going to join us, Father Phelan?" the parish
priest enquired loudly. "Or is it too early for you? Your father
perhaps taught you that a gentleman never drinks before seven
o'clock." The unrestrained bitterness of his voice, the desire to
wantonly wound was appallingly evident to all present.

Father Phelan appeared to reel but recovered himself
sufficiently to assume some of his characteristic flamboyance.
"Ah no, Canon. My father, God rest him, would drink at the
crack of dawn if cows yielded whiskey instead of milk." There
was an appreciative titter. "As for me, I took the pledge some
years ago and God's been good to me. I haven't broken it yet. But
of course I'll have a tonic and drink to your health. It would be
boorish of me not to."

He stared intently at Father Phelan's back as the man opened a
bottle. His hands were trembling. He managed to pour sufficient,
spilling a great deal as he did so. It splashed down his cassock. He
wiped it off laughing uncertainly. "Your very good health,
Canon," he said, raising his glass.

"Your very good health, Father, and forgive my scurrilous
remarks. They were quite uncalled for and wholly unjust. Please
forgive me."

"No offence, Canon, no offence."

A silence fell. Everyone glanced at everyone else and then
looked elsewhere. He felt like the proverbial stranger at the feast.
The old priest laid aside his glass and turned to the commandant:
"Mrs O'Sullivan I take it has prepared a fine meal for you. I'm
sure you are all hungry after such a strenuous morning. You will
have to excuse me, I'm afraid. I have some pressing matters to
attend to." There were token protests from both the officers and
genuine regrets from Father Good. He silenced them with a wave
of his hand. "You will all have to forgive me. Father Phelan I
know will prove an admirable host, as he has done in the past."
He nodded to the company. Both officers shook his hand in

farewell and again expressed their regrets that he could not remain. He wished them well and left.

He helped himself into his overcoat. Unaccountably, despite the intense heat of the day, he felt a chill. He was about to leave the house when Father Phelan entered the hall from the sitting room. "The keys, Canon," he said uncertainly. "You'll be needing the keys." He offered a number of cumbersome keys of various kinds on a large metal keyholder. They were unwieldly and far too awkward to carry about. Nevertheless he recognised the offer for what it was: submission. He declined to accept them. "I would feel happier if you were to retain them, Father, and I would be obliged if you were to continue being responsible for the parish as you have in the immediate past. I must confess to some uncertainty and indeed confusion. Please oblige me in this matter. I would be most grateful."

The curate swallowed hard and nodded, plainly gratified. "As you wish, Canon, as you wish." He was about to open the door when Father Phelan exclaimed: "Canon!" He sounded anxious and afraid.

"I am only going for a short walk, Father. I shall not be very long. Please do not be concerned. Everything is quite well." And he passed through the portals of the house door for the first time in many years. Pausing on the uppermost step of the flight down to the path, he breathed deeply. Bran came bounding from behind the house. He yelped and snapped, sniffed him suspiciously and then slunk away.

Flags and bunting were to be seen everywhere. The streets were deserted. A calmness prevailed. He gazed at the town. The three protestant churches, each with a proud and defiant steeple. The convent grounds to the northwest now totally deserted. People everywhere were having their midday meal. For most of those who had participated in the morning's events and had most likely been fasting since midnight of the night before, food and drink would be very welcome.

Slowly he began to go down. Beneath his feet were scattered the petals of flowers which had been taken from gilded baskets by young girls in white communion dresses. Having kissed them they were strewn beneath the feet of the priest carrying the monstrance. Readily recognisable were the petal of roses and marguerites and the lesser but nevertheless beautiful petals of wild flowers. Just above the statue of the Virgin holding the Christ Child the steps divided and flanked the level on which the statue stood. The temporary altar had been erected directly in front of the statue. It had been stripped of its magnificent cloths and stood bare and stark, its white paint reflecting harshly in the strong sunlight.

He heard the sound of childish laughter as he approached. Quietly descending the steps, he saw that bare-footed children in dirty clothes were aping the service of benediction. One stout fellow with a strong sense of bravado was kneeling on the uppermost step of the altar and chanting gibberish, meant to be the latin of the ceremony. A few boys and girls were kneeling further back, laughing and giggling and parodying the responses. They all had marks of poverty. Ungainly development, pallid complexions and various blemishes. One girl with lively dark eyes and a head of auburn hair had a squint in her eye which destroyed her otherwise defined beauty. They were, he knew, outcasts. The poverty of their families meant that they were unable to clothe or shoe them presentably and parental pride would not allow the children to take part in the morning's ceremonies which were striking and colourful and the source of innocent wonder and beauty to the young children. They froze in position when they saw him and lapsed into fearful silence. He raised his hand in salute and left them to their simple game. Blighted, he thought bitterly, now you can at least recognise blight in others and know that all human failing is not a simple matter of defeat of the will.

He passed down the main street over which several arches of evergreens had been erected, each bearing white banners on which suitably eucharistic aspirations had been painted. By Crowley's bootshop he came upon a family group. A man in dark, unsuitably heavy clothing. A woman, once beautiful but even now still striking in a fine womanly way, was fussing affectionately over a child in white communion dress and wearing a veil and headband of delicate miniature waxen lillies. She carried a large decorative wicker basket painted in vivid gold with big white ribbons trailing from a silken bow on the handle, marking her as one of the select — usually chosen from the better families in town — who walked before the canopy strewing flowers in homage to the host.

On approaching nearer he saw that the man was holding a box camera. They became quiet on seeing him. Their eyes darted about in alarm. The man appeared as if trying to decide which way lay his best escape. The woman hesitated, then took charge of the situation. She held herself erect and commandingly greeted him with simple sincerity and altogether without fear: "Good afternoon, Canon. A beautiful day, thank God, for the procession."

He raised his biretta in agreement. When he passed the group

the girl in white shrunk into her father as if threatened by danger.
He glimpsed behind them an altar of unusual magnificence,
erected in the well between the shop windows, both of which had
their blinds drawn. A statue of the Child of Prague, which usually
struck him as clownish or dollish, stood above a profusion of
banked flowers of all colours. The statue was of fine porcelain
and painted by a craftsman of undoubted skill. It was obviously a
product of a continental country notable for its porcelain, rather
than the more common hideous plaster image invariably the
product of some Italian firm. Father and child he could see were
frightened by him. Only the generous and womanly mother was
without fear. It pained to see a child cower before his very
shadow.

He crossed the bridge. A stiff wind was blowing upstream and
provided relief from the unremitting heat of the direct sunshine.
In the middle of the bridge a giant arch had been erected. It bore a
banner with a golden rayed monstrance in its centre and the
legend 'Christ Our Only King'. The sectarian emphasis was not
lost on him. He thought it childish and somewhat mean. To his
delight the river was low. The waters ran rillingly between huge
white stones smoothened by water and shaped like the humps of
camels. He passed onto Mill Street. Here as elsewhere bunting
and flags were fluttering. In some places altars were being
dismantled and through the open doorways came the smell of
roasting meat. He felt his stomach respond and realised that he
had had no food for sometime. He met some people. They
greeted him cautiously and with some surprise. One woman
entered her house and slammed the door shut in what was
intended as an open snub.

He reached Copley's Lane. The sight of the houses stirred him
deeply. He again thought of the smiling girl and the
uncontrollable veil. Her image remained in his mind for some
seconds and then was gone. Some short distance down the lane he
paused, struck with horror. The house in which the Maddens had
lived was unoccupied and had all the unhappy appearance of a
house long abandoned. Its windows were shuttered. Its door
stoutly boarded up with planks of wood. The garden was a mass
of tangled rose growths, high pernicious grass and prolific, ever
thriving montbretia. Silence and summer warmth enshrouded
the entire scene. Too dumbstruck to move, he remained staring
for some time.

"Yourself, Canon. Faith and it's good to see you up and about
the place. Is it the Maddens you were looking for now?"

He started and found himself confronted by an old woman, a

shawl drawn up about her head, possibly as a mark of respect. She smiled and her question had been politely, ingratiatingly asked, but there was a strong strain of suppressed excitement in her voice.

"I had thought to visit them, yes."

She clucked sympathetically. Her mottled hand toyed with the folds of her shawl. "Poor man. He was near demented when herself died. Mrs Madden that is. She didn't last long, poor creature, when Catherine died. Never recovered. Broke her heart entirely. She shrank away to nothing. Did you know that, Canon?"

"No, I am afraid I did not."

"Then it looked as if the same thing was going to happen to him, so one day he just walked out of the house and left it, lock, stock and barrel. Mr Hosfurd, that's the landlord, had the place barred and bolted and has been looking for the man everywhere since. Isn't that strange?"

"It is, Madam, very strange indeed. If you will forgive me now, I must go." He turned unsteadily, fearing at any moment that he might faint, and began to retrace his footsteps up the laneway.

"You're more than welcome to a cup of tea, Canon. I'll wet the pot for you. It won't take a minute."

He turned to her. "Thank you. That is very kind of you but I think not. Thank you."

She licked her lips nervously, hurt showing on her face, less dismay, he thought, than the look of a schemer thwarted.

He felt inexpressibly old and weary and now regretted his decision to visit the house. He found the heat unbearable and judiciously kept to the shaded side of the streets as he slowly and not without difficulty made his way back to the parochial house. To his annoyance he found he had no key and could not therefore enter the house unobtrusively, as he wished to do.

Mrs O'Sullivan admitted him. "Commandant Kelly would like you to join them, Canon."

From the parlour came the sound of rather loud but happy conversation. The commandant was relating some of his military experiences. He shook his head. "Later perhaps, Mrs O'Sullivan, but not now."

"You wouldn't like the drop of tea, or maybe a drink?"

He hesitated. "I think not. If I change my mind I can always ring."

"Very well." She watched him with some concern while he mounted the stairs.

He entered his room and gladly sank into an armchair. The

folly of what he had done overwhelmed him. Even if both parents were still alive and living still in their home, what could he possibly have expected to gain from such a visit? He would have hardly been welcomed, he who had been so closely associated with their daughter in her last illness. He longed to sleep but could not. He was far too disturbed and too tired in spirit. The long tenebrous night was over. He had emerged not into the bright light of that promissory Easter morning but into the grey light of sad, indigent day. He would now have to live as circumstances would best permit him. He would renounce all priestly vows and forego all priestly duties. His love of her would be as a wound deep and ever grievous. He would have to bear it all the days of his life, as he would have to bear all other things.